Acknowledgments

D1329788

To my awesome family for

supporting me every step of

the way, I couldn't have done

this without you!!!

Chapter One

A woman walked along the street of Pease Avenue. Her hair was up in a tight bun on the top of her head. Bright blue butterflies circled it, never leaving. They matched her dress, a blue ball gown. *That* was strange. It was pouring, but not a drop touched her. Magic? No, magic wasn't real. Then could it be? What kind of machine blew the rain away from you if you didn't have an umbrella? Or kept butterflies circling your hair? The woman looked to be in her late forties. If magic was real, she'd be a fairy godmother. Pushing along two strollers, the woman looked anxiously back over her shoulder, sensing somebody watching her.

In the first stroller was a girl and a boy. The girl had short black hair, looking to be about two and the boy had dark brown hair and looked three-ish. The other stroller held another boy and a girl. The boy had super light blond hair and so did the girl. They seemed like twins and couldn't be one yet. All were asleep, and the twins were drooling non stop.

The woman hurried along, seeming to be looking for a certain house. There were no lights on in any of them. Well, except for a small one at the very end of the street. Outside of that house on the porch was a young woman reading on a rocking chair, although she was barely getting any light. The older woman ran up to her, nearly crashing the strollers in her haste. The two greeted each other and had a brief whispered conversation. There was no need to whisper because nobody was out at this time of day, and yet the women both seemed too tense.

In the end the older woman gave the younger woman a letter and laid the crib carefully at her feet. She let go of the stroller, gently kissing each of the sleeping children on the top of the head and departed. Once the older woman was out of sight the young woman gave a disgusted look to each of the children. She proceeded to put the crib and stroller inside.

Thirteen years went by fast and nothing more unusual happened. Well nothing that anybody really knew about. Inside number 35 Pease Ave however it was a different story. Inside the four siblings were having a *very* unusual conversation.

"Jake you *have* to tell someone," Conner was urging his older brother from his spot on the beanbag chair.

"No," Jake replied curtly, lying face up on the floor, hands behind his head. His homework lay forgotten next to him.

"But Jake, we don't know what this is!" said Isabella, waving her hands, annoyed, from the top bunk, her legs hanging down.

"And we don't know what it could do to you," added Jessica, scrolling through her phone, casually. She didn't seem that bothered by the conversation.

"Well I feel fine and absolutely nothing has happened to me," argued Jake.

"Yet," sighed Conner. But he let it go.

"Besides, controlling weather is pretty cool," Jake said.

"But you can only control the weather when you get angry and you can't *actually* control it," said Jessica, liking someone's Instagram photo.

It was true. Whenever Jake had gotten angry in the past few weeks he created weather outside, which was both good and bad (though mostly bad). Once he realized that he was changing the weather he snapped out of it. There had been one particular day when the wind had blown open the window and blew a heavy chair onto Izzy's leg. It had been an unusually strong wind. Thankfully, it had not hurt her seriously. Nobody else but the four siblings had been around when any of the incidents happened.

Without anything else to say, Jake returned to his homework. Izzy jumped down from the bunk bed and went back to working on her soccer skills. Conner grabbed his book from the ground while Jess continued to look through social media.

Just then the door opened and a middle aged, skinny, mousy haired lady appeared in the doorway. "I couldn't help but overhearing and it *sounds* as though you were arguing," she said, "May I have to remind you that one of the most important rules in this house is that you absolutely can not argue. *Especially* when I have a headache."

"Sorry Ms. Mafore," Izzy apologized, sounding extremely insincere.

"Don't apologize, just don't do it," snapped Ms. Mafore. "I hope you did your homework," she added as an afterthought.

When she left and couldn't hear them anymore Jess and Izzy started bickering.

"Izzy can you not be so loud, I'm *trying* to apply my makeup."

"Well, I'm working on my soccer skills so I'm ready for the game Sunday," Isabella replied.

"Um Iz, tomorrow is Sunday," Conner chimed in, looking up from his book.

"Exactly," said Isabella, glaring at Jess.

"Well," said Jessica, with an air of superiority, "I have a date with Matt tomorrow and I want to look my best."

"I thought you were dating Brandon," Conner said, puzzled. With Jess it was hard to keep track.

"Not anymore. But Matt will dump *me* if I don't look my best," Jess said, turning around to glare at Izzy.

"Could you not argue while I'm doing my homework?" Jake asked but he was ignored.

"Well let's see what makes sense," said Izzy in a mocking voice, "Is your date tonight? No, so why would you be putting on makeup right now?"

"I want to practice some new looks to see if I like them better than my old ones. Besides I'm older than you so you have to listen to *me*," Jess retorted.

"*Please* stop argu—," begged Jake but he was cut off.

"Well you don't have to be rude about it!" said Izzy, her voice slowly rising. "All I wanted to do was practice my soccer skills because we have a big game against Agawam tomorrow. That's West Springfield's rival in case *you* didn't know. And even if you're older than Conner and I, Jake is still the oldest and *he* can tell *you* what to do." That was ironic, because neither one of them was actually listening to Jake.

Completely ignoring the last thing Izzy had said Jess replied, "Of course I know who

West Springfield's rival is. Matt's soccer team is playing them Thursday."

"Why does everything have to be about your boyfriends!? Why can't you pay attention to your siblings for *once*. In case you didn't notice, we've been to every single one of your boyfriends' games, which is hard since they change *weekly* and you haven't been to a *single* one of our games. Not one of my soccer games and none of Conner's baseball *or* soccer games," Izzy was almost to the point of yelling, and Jake really couldn't stand it.

"Can you guys please stop arguing for one second, I'm *trying* to concentrate!" Jake nearly shouted, but again he was ignored.

"It's not my fault if all my dates happen to be on the same day," Jess said, finally looking up from her mirror.

"You make sure that your dates are on the same days and at the same time as our games," Izzy fumed.

This had gone on too long for Jake. He was getting really mad that they weren't listening to him. He usually wouldn't get mad this easily, but the morning had just been grating his nerves. His eyes started to glow yellow and thunder boomed in the distance. Jake sat up from the floor as the power within him swirled like a tornado.

"Hey!" Conner yelled, as his book flew out of his reach. The windows crashed open and an angry wind blew inside. The ragged bean bag chair Conner was sitting on flew out from under him. Everything got lifted up in the air except for the people. Izzy fought her way to the window and slammed it shut, but it was useless because it just opened again.

"Oh *no*," Jess muttered. She was lifted up in the air by the wind and was slammed against the wall. Once everything was swirling in the air Jake realized what he was doing and stopped. Conner's bean bag chair fell on top of him but he didn't get hurt, unlike Jess.

"Oh god, JESS!" Jake yelled. He scrambled over to her and carefully leaned her against the wall. She had been knocked unconscious, but didn't seem to have any injuries.

Izzy smiled mischievously as she pulled black, blue, red, and beige Sharpies from her nightstand, which was still standing upright in its original position. Her nightstand had not been flung around the room during the storm with the other furniture because it was glued to the ground. She learned from Jake's previous weather fiascos that in order to keep her precious drawing materials from being wrecked, she had to be proactive. She loved art almost as much as she loved soccer and didn't want any harm done to her materials. With sharpies, colored pencils, and Jess's eyeshadow in hand, she leaned over Jessica and started drawing. When she was done Jess had two realistic black eyes and an expertly drawn mustache.

Conner stared, open mouthed at her. "She's going to kill you when she wakes up," Conner told Izzy, trying to hide his grin at his twin's expert work.

"Well then, I guess we'll just have to keep it a secret," said Jake. "Here, help me lift her in bed so she'll think the storm was just a dream." Grabbing her by the shoulders he gestured for Izzy to grab her legs.

Conner had already repositioned his bean bag chair and started reading. Jake thought he heard Izzy mutter, "Well that's what you get for arguing with me, miss *princess.*"

Just before they got to her bed, they laid her down on the floor. Jake went up the ladder from the bottom of his bunk to Jess's. Jake and Jess shared a bunk bed, while Conner and Izzy shared another. At first Izzy and Jess had shared a bunk, but that had quickly turned into a disaster. They all had to share a room. This probably wasn't the best solution, as they had space downstairs, and another room upstairs, but Ms. Mafore *loved* to make things hard for them. So, they all had to share one room. Izzy complained frequently, but it never changed.

Jake hoisted Jess up by the arms and Izzy grabbed her legs and pushed them up. In the process, Jess's head smacked against the ceiling, but she didn't stir.

"Be careful," Conner warned.

"We are," they called in unison.

They finally got Jess up onto her bunk.

"Whew", said Izzy wiping the imaginary sweat off her forehead and jumping down. "Now I can practice my soccer skills uninterrupted," she added, throwing a nasty glance at Jess who by now had started to snore loudly.

A knock at the door made them turn. It opened and a brown haired, skinny looking little girl walked in picking her nose. Behind her came her mother, who was the owner of the house, and the siblings' substitute mother.

"Edel," she said gesturing to her daughter who was still picking her nose, "has bedbugs again so she will have to take your room tonight," Ms. Mafore informed them.

"But that's not fair," said Jake outraged, "It's always me who has to sleep in the living room because I'm the oldest—"

Ms. Mafore cut him off and informed him, "And I've decided that *all* of you will be sleeping in the living room. Also, clean up this room, it looks like a bomb went off in here," she added, surveying the overturned desk and scattered books.

"If only you knew," Izzy muttered.

"What was that?"

"Nothing."

Jess let out a rumbling snore and Ms. Mafore took that as her cue to leave. She spun around and Edel followed. Before she left Edel stuck her tongue out at them and stomped on a loose floorboard so that all of the Sharpies on Izzy's desk tumbled to the ground. Edel, looking satisfied, skipped out of the room.

Chapter Two

Jess got up, yawned, stretched and looked over the top of the bunk wearily.

"How did I get here?"she asked Conner who was closest, but reading. When he reads, barely anything gets to him. Deciding that she probably climbed up in bed and fell asleep, she let it go and started climbing down. She didn't remember anything that had happened. Izzy and Jake immediately started hiding their laughs with their hands.

"What's so funny?" Jess demanded.

"Oh nothing," said Izzy, quickly going back to juggling her soccer ball.

"Hey Jess?" said Conner, coming out from behind his book and laughing, "you might want to look in the mirror."

Jess, looking suspiciously at Izzy, walked outside to the bathroom. They strained their ears to hear her but didn't have to. Soon they heard an ear splitting shriek and Izzy started laughing hysterically.

Jess stormed into the room. She knew Izzy did it because of her guilty face. If looks could kill, Izzy would be long gone.

"WHAT," she screamed, "DID YOU DO!?"

Izzy, a bit startled by Jess's towering rage, stammered, "Well. . . um. . . I. . . I just thought it would be kind of funny."

"YOU THOUGHT IT WOULD BE FUNNY IF I SHOWED UP AT SCHOOL MONDAY AND LOOKED LIKE A—," she tried to think exactly what she looked like.

Izzy, trying to distract her, said, "Just so you know we're all sleeping in the living room tonight because Edel has bed bugs in her bed again," she rolled her eyes, "And," she added, "We have to clean up our room."

Jess surveying the room thought it looked much messier than usual. The desk was overturned, while books, drawing materials, makeup, and school papers were scattered on the floor.

"Oh . . . um," said Jake, struggling to think of a story about what had happened.

Izzy came to his rescue. "I had lost something and went crazy looking for it." They couldn't believe that Jess had forgotten about the wind.

"Oh, okay." Jess said and she started cleaning up. In about thirty seconds she was done. Conner looking up from his book told Jess she was a neat freak because she had finished so fast.

Jess shrugged modestly. Conner went back to reading. Jess walked out, aiming to wash away all the stuff on her face in the sink, throwing Izzy a look that said she wouldn't forget. Izzy, grinning in response to it, took out a sketchpad and started drawing. Jake took out his chromebook to start typing his essay.

After about an hour, Ms. Mafore came back in and told them dinner would be ready in five minutes. "Well," said Conner after she left, "We should probably start hiding our stuff so Edel doesn't find it."

"And grab all the stuff we need for tonight," Izzy added.

Jake and Jess agreed, so Conner pulled up part of the carpet and took out a couple loose floorboards which uncovered a big dirt hole. In the hole was a huge treasure chest. Not the real fancy ones that rich people buy, this one was made out of cheap plastic.

They had bought it at a Dollar General in town for a price of $17.99. That may seem expensive, but it was huge. They actually got it cheap. They had bought it for occasions like this. The first time Edel had been in their room alone a lot of things were ruined. Izzy's best drawings in her sketchpad had been scribbled on with black sharpie. Most pages in Conner's books had been torn out and scattered on the ground.

Jake's best tests were all arranged in a folder neatly and the grades had been colored on. Edel also wrote failing scores on them. Jess's lipstick was swapped with lip gloss, which everybody knows she despises ("Why put anything on your lips if you can't see it?") They had learned their lesson with Edel. They all got their most valuable things and hid them in the chest. Jess took a cardboard box down from a shelf and took out things like rubix cubes, fidget spinners, scrunchies, slime, notepads, and some books to keep Edel busy so she wouldn't find where all their stuff went.

While Izzy tried to find some spare markers and crayons, Jess found some more stuff to put out for Edel. Conner and Jake took blue sheets off their beds and put pink frilly sheets in their place. Then they put light blue pillows on top of the bed.

They did this because every time Edel saw even a corner of their regular sheets (even if she wasn't sleeping on that bed) she started having a fit. (Why? They had no idea but they weren't complaining). Imagine coming back to your bed knowing somebody who picks their own nose has slept on it. So they had to go through a lot of work to get the room prepared for her. It was a lot of work to do, but they've done it so many times, so now it was easy.

"WHERE ARE YOU!? DIDN'T I SAY DINNER WAS IN FIVE MINUTES!?" Ms. Mafore screamed. The siblings exchanged irritated glances and then hurried out of the room.

Dinner was dry toast and strawberries for Jess, Conner, Izzy and Jake. While Edel and her mom enjoyed steak, mashed potatoes, corn, and hot rolls. Ms. Mafore only did this to try and get a rise out of them. After they did that she would punish them. The siblings would angrily respond once in a while.

Jess, Conner, Jake, and Izzy excused themselves to finish preparing their room for Edel. Looking through the closet Jess found some old, squished, and dusty board games like Monopoly, which they knew was Edel's favorite board game.

Conner and Jake finished making the beds just as Izzy found a thirty six pack of crayons and some old markers. She put them out as Jake and Conner hopped down from the beds. Now that they were done preparing for Edel it was time for them to pack their stuff.

They got out some worn sleeping bags for Jake and Conner (Jess and Izzy would sleep on the couch). Conner also got a huge book as Izzy got a sketchpad and a pencil, while Jess got a mini mirror and some makeup. Jake brought his laptop and, always thinking ahead, brought some junk food, flashlights, and a sweatshirt for each of them.

Each sibling also brought a pillow and some blankets. Finally they were ready and it only took them about two hours (Jess was a super slow packer and was always losing things). They dragged all their stuff down to the living room.

Ms. Mafore told them once they were out there, they could watch something if they found the controller. She left and the siblings started looking for the remote. After a few minutes Izzy found it under a couch cushion. "Score!" she said, "I found the remote and five bucks! I'm picking what we're going to watch." After a few seconds of mindlessly flipping through channels, she found a Star Wars and a Marvel movie.

"Hmmm. Let's see. Should we watch Marvel or Star Wars?" she asked Conner.

"Definitely Marvel," Conner told her.

"Can't we watch something like a high school drama or a romance movie for once?" asked Jess.

"No way, action is so much better than *romance*," said Conner pretending to vomit.

"Oh well," dramatically sighed Jess.

"I like Star Wars, I think that we should watch that," said Jake.

"Yeah I guess Star Wars is pretty good, not as good as Marvel, but I would watch it," agreed Conner.

"All in favor of Star Wars, raise your hand," Izzy said, sitting on the couch to count. Conner and Jake raised their hands. "All in favor of a *romance* movie raise your hand," Izzy called out, rolling her eyes at Jess who had put both of her hands up. "The votes are in and the winner is," she paused dramatically for effect, "Star Wars!"

"Yay!" loudly whispered Conner and Jake.

"Fine," grumbled Jess, "but next time we're watching what I want to watch."

"Okay, that's fair," agreed Conner.

"Just start the movie Izzy," Jake told her, "while I get out some food." He started pulling out twinkies, mini cupcakes, and oreos out of the backpack he brought.

"Oh, gimmie," demanded Izzy, who was addicted to junk food. Jake passed her some twinkies, gave Conner a few mini cupcakes, and Jess a big pack of oreos. For himself he revealed a big, chocolate chip, fudge covered brownie. It looked amazing. "Awww no fair! How come you get the brownie?" Izzy pouted.

"Because I'm the oldest and most important," teased Jake.

"Yeah, right," snorted Izzy.

"Iz," Conner complained. "Start the movie!"

"Okay, okay, if you insist," said Izzy, pressing on the channel, and tossing the remote. The movie started and everybody dove into their snacks.

After the movie Izzy checked the time on her watch and asked, "It's only ten, should we stay up until eleven, ten thirty, or just go to bed now?"

"We should definitely go to bed now. I need my beauty sleep."

"Oh, jeez. The beauty queen needs her rest. All hail the beauty queen," Izzy chanted mockingly, bowing down low, "I think we should go to bed at eleven."

"You have a soccer game at seven thirty tomorrow Izzy,," Jake reminded her. "We should probably go to bed at ten thirty because you have to be there at seven in the morning and it will take us about forty five to get there on our bikes, so we would have to leave around six fifteen."

"Okay," Izzy agreed, "I guess that's reasonable, but you have to come Jess."

"Okay, okay, fine. If you insist," she told them, surprising everybody. "But I get the last cup of oatmeal tomorrow!"

"Sure, whatever," said Izzy, just glad she was coming.

Chapter Three

"Come on Izzy, come on!" yelled Conner, cheering for his sister on the sidelines.

Izzy was sprinting up the field, dribbling the soccer ball, being chased by the whole other team.

"Teacher's pet," whispered somebody behind Conner. He turned around and saw his least favorite person: Thomas Davies. Thomas Davies was the meanest, most selfish, most obnoxious, most cocky person he knew. He was about to say something but realized that Thomas wasn't talking to him, he was talking to Jake.

"Shut up Thomas," muttered Jake.

"Oh, is the little teacher's pet finally sticking up for himself," mocked Thomas in a baby voice.

"*Leave*, Thomas," Jake said.

"Uhh, no," laughed Thomas.

"Thomas, either say something worthwhile, which we both know you can't, or leave now," Conner snapped.

"I was talking to your loser brother, not you, nerd" growled Thomas.

Conner rolled his eyes, not hurt in the least, but Jake wasn't liking this one bit. "Go back to the rock you were living in the first place," said Jake, his voice steadier now that he was angry.

"I'd like to see you or your nerdy brother make me."

The crowd roared, it seemed that Izzy had just scored a goal. Jake was getting mad about the taunts that Thomas kept making about Conner. "Hey, Jake? Izzy just scored a goal!" interrupted Jess who had been looking down at her phone for the past ten minutes and chose now to involve herself in the conversation.

But Jake wasn't paying attention. His eyes started turning yellow and in the distance you could see the beginning of a small tornado. Thomas had turned around right before Jake's eyes started turning yellow and was now gawking at the tornado in the distance. A startling wind swept in, knocking Thomas and his friends to the ground. While looking back with panicked glances, they took off running.

Unfortunately even though Jake's eyes had stopped glowing and he was out of his trance, the tornado was still there. He looked around in terror of what was happening. He knew he had to either get everybody out of there or get it under control. He went with the first option. Cupping his hands around his mouth he started yelling.

"Hey!" nobody even gave him a glance. "HEY!" He tried again and this time everybody stopped what they were doing and looked at him. "THERE IS A TORNADO COMING HERE

RIGHT NOW," he pointed to the tornado and everybody started screaming and running in the opposite direction of it. Panic and fear overwhelmed Jake.

"IZZY! IZZY!" he yelled, panicking at the thought of what might have happened to her. She may have gone to the bathroom and doesn't know about the tornado or maybe she was trampled. He was hoping she had already gone with everybody else to the parking lot. But Jake knew that was probably too much to ask for. "I'm here! I'm here!" came a voice behind Jake.

"Oh Izzy, thank God," Jake muttered while hugging her.

"Jeez, personal space," said Izzy, who's not big on affection, but this time she let it go. Jake let go of her and Conner said, "Um, guys? You know I hate to break this up but you're missing the fact that there is a TORNADO heading STRAIGHT FOR US!"

"Oh. Right. Well let's go!" Izzy cried. They took off sprinting as the tornado kept coming closer and closer. Once they were at the parking lot they quickly unlocked their bikes and took off. They managed to keep ahead of it and got home. Looking back they saw the tornado far in the distance, but coming closer.

Once they returned home, the siblings ran inside and saw the news on the TV reporting, "Everybody, we have about fifteen minutes before the tornado comes." Ms. Mafore instructed, "I want you to get your most personal belongings and bring them downstairs. I'll turn the heat on down there and bring some food. Do it quickly. NOW!"

The siblings and Edel ran into their rooms to gather their most prized possessions. Each grabbing a backpack, the siblings pulled up the loose floorboard and opened the chest. Izzy grabbed her sketchbook, phone, her signed soccer ball by all her teammates, and art materials. Conner grabbed a bunch of books, his phone, and airpods. Jake got his best scoring tests, report cards, laptop, phone, and some junk food. Jess got makeup, her phone, and a mirror.

After everything was packed, Jake opened the closet and threw out a bunch of sleeping bags, blankets, and their pillows. They tore off downstairs bringing all their items with them. Once all their stuff was downstairs they ran back into the kitchen with another backpack and helped Ms. Mafore pack food. They saw Edel with a bulging backpack running downstairs, her thumb now in her mouth instead of up her nose.

Finally, with three backpacks pressing down on anybody who carried them because of their weight, the siblings and Ms. Mafore headed downstairs. Downstairs there was a bigger room and a closet which could barely fit two people. The room was cold and had windows at the very top of the walls, which would most definitely break if a tornado ever passed by. Guess which one the siblings got? The one *without* heat and *had* windows. Grumbling, Jess, Conner, Izzy, and Jake stalked into the cold room.

They closed the door behind them and started setting up their sleeping bags as far away from the window as possible.

"Jake," said Izzy, taking a deep breath. "The tornado is like two minutes away from us! You have to stop it or we could die."

The reality of the situation sunk in.

"Umm, I could try," closing his eyes tightly, he started muttering. He opened them back up and asked, "Did it work?" Checking her phone, Jess answered by turning up the volume on the news and shushing them.

"Breaking news. A tornado seems to be coming towards West Springfield right now. Weathermen and women are befuddled.

Incoming." He paused to listen to something in his ear, "It seems to be heading towards Pease Avenue. Stay inside and do not come out until you get news that this crisis is over. Back to you Sherry."

Now a different person came on to the screen, in a news office this time. "Thanks Ted," she said to the man, "I just happen to have somebody who witnessed this tornado here at the studio." She grabbed somebody with her hand off screen and pulled them on. "Thomas *Davies*," gasped Conner who was quickly shushed by Izzy. Thomas was pushed onto the screen by somebody off stage. He grinned arrogantly. "Uh yeah. Hi my name is Thomas Davies and I witnessed this crisis. So I was standing there at the soccer game talking to my buddy. Then suddenly, out of nowhere, I turned around to cheer for our team, who was about to score by the way, and I saw a huge tornado coming straight for me!" He shudders as if remembering it. Then he started to really exaggerate.

"And then the wind knocked a nice old lady down so I helped her up. Next, I started yelling so people would know what was happening. Once I got their attention I pointed to the tornado. Everybody started running towards the parking lot. After I made sure that everybody was safe, risking my own life I might add, the tornado was almost right behind me! I started sprinting to the exit. It's a good thing I'm a fast runner. I just barely made it home alive." He was *way* over-exaggerating this.

"Wow! What a story," Sherry told Thomas. "Now, back to you Ted."

At this point, Jess turned her phone off. Even though he knew he couldn't do anything about it Conner was still super ticked off about Thomas saying those things. Thomas didn't even stick around to tell anybody about the tornado, much less be the last one there helping everybody. He really didn't like it when jerks, like Thomas, took all the credit.

But again he had to remind himself that there was nothing he could do about it so he should just let it go. The tornado was right outside the house anyway. Wait. The tornado was right outside the window! "JAKE!" Conner yelled. The windows shattered and glass shards flew towards the siblings like daggers. Izzy screamed as one slashed her in the arm. Closing his eyes Jake concentrated as hard as he could. Panic was rising inside of him, but he pushed it down. He *had* to stop this, or they could get hurt. Or worse, killed.

"Come on. Come on," he thought, just as what felt like a needle pierced his arm. His concentration broke, he looked up to see the tornado sort of blow away into the sky and then evaporate into the wind.

"Everybody okay?" asked Jake, yanking the sliver of glass out of his arm.

"Yup," mumbled Jess.

He got a weak okay from Izzy. The piece of glass had just skimmed her and she was not seriously injured but would still need a band aid. Everybody turned to Conner and horrifyingly saw a piece of glass sticking out of his leg and wrist. "Umm I think I might need a band aid," he said weakly. Blood was starting to pool around him.

"MS. MAFORE!" Jess screamed.

"Oh. My. God," Ms. Mafore said once she saw Conner, "That is going to cost a lot of money to fix."

"But you will get him fixed right?" Izzy asked.

"Umm… "

"RIGHT!?"

"Yes. I guess. Jessica dial 911."

Her phone slipping between her fingers Jess dialed the number. "This is 911. What is your emergency?"

"It's my brother. He's got glass shards in him from the window and tornado," answered Jess, her voice shaking.

"Address."

"Thirty five Pease Ave."

"Okay stay put I'm sending help right now."

"Bye."

Meanwhile Izzy and Conner were trying to stop the flow of blood streaming out of Conner's body. In a few minutes the sound of sirens filled the air. Ms. Mafore ran up to open the door for the people. Heavy boots stomped downstairs and firefighters appeared. A couple of men helped Conner get up and start walking towards the stairs."We can go with him into the hospital and ambulance right?" Izzy asked one of the men.

"Is he your brother?"

"We are all his siblings. Except her," Jake said, gesturing to Edel.

"And," Jess added, "That woman is not his mother."

"Just let us go," pleaded Izzy

"Fine," the man reluctantly agreed.

Scrambling back up the stairs after their brother, Izzy stopped Edel and Ms. Mafore. "This is all your fault," she growled, "If you had just let us all be in the same room together none of this would have happened. And one day you will have to pay for all the evil things you have done to us."

Glaring coldly at Izzy, Ms. Mafore told her, "Oh I highly doubt that. One day soon *you* will get what's coming to *you*."

Before either of them could say anything else, they were called upstairs. Izzy hurried upstairs and out the front door. Jake and the man helped Conner into the back of the ambulance. Conner winced in pain, trying to hide it. Jess and Izzy climbed into the back of the ambulance with Conner and Jake. Once everybody was in and secure they sped off towards the hospital.

Conner was rushed out of sight as soon as they walked into the hospital door. They all took a seat in the waiting room. Ms. Mafore was asked to sign some papers and Edel went over to the kids' side of the waiting room, sticking her finger up her nose as she went. Izzy put her head in her hands and Jess put a comforting arm around her.

A minute later a smaller, plump woman, with a kind looking face came in, her gray hair in a bun on top of her head. "I gotta admit I don't like the uniforms here," Jess whispered to Izzy, trying to make her sister feel better. All the hospital people were wearing an off-white jacket with black pants and a white shirt. Around their waists were small clips with hand sanitizer, tissues, and other doctor equipment.

The lady walked over to their group and Jake and Jess could have sworn they had seen

that lady before. She looked so familiar. Ms.
Mafore gave the lady a cold look.

"My name's Amelia," she said, offering
them all hand sanitizer "You are Conner
Mitchell's family, right?"

"Yes," Jake answered. A sudden rush of
guilt enveloped him. This was *his* fault. And if
Conner wasn't okay...

Amelia smiled warmly. "He's going to be
fine. You can see him now," she informed them.
Relief flooded Jake, but the guilt was still there.

"We will," Izzy told her. Ms. Mafore
started to walk forward, but Amelia stopped
her. "*Family* only," she said. Ms. Mafore glared at
her. Amelia led them to the elevator. "Floor
three, room 376. All the way to the right."

"Okay. Thanks." The siblings took the
elevator and walked to the right. They found
room 376 and Izzy quietly knocked on the door.
"Come in," they heard someone say. They
carefully opened the door and walked inside.

There they saw Conner on a bed, wearing a hospital gown. Next to him was the same lady who told them which room he was in. How did she get there so fast?

The siblings gave her a quizzical look. "Hey guys," Conner greeted them.

"Hi Conner. How ya feeling?" Izzy asked.

He shrugged, "I've felt better."

Jake glanced down at the floor, looking guilty and embarrassed.

"It's okay Jake. It wasn't your fault," Conner told his brother, when Jake didn't look convinced, he tried again, his voice harder. "It *wasn't*."

Jake gave Conner a weak smile. Then a man in a white coat walked in, clipboard in his hand.

"You are the siblings of Conner right?" he asked.

"Yep," Jess answered.

"Okay. He's going to need crutches. Just as a precaution. He will also need a splint for both his hand and his leg."

"Thanks Doc. He's not going to spend the night is he?" Izzy asked.

"Yes, unfortunately. But he's healing up unusually fast." The doctor paused. "Well actually it's like nothing we've seen before."

"What do you mean?" Conner asked him.

"I mean that in just a day or two, or maybe even less, all that will be left of his injury is a scar. And if you're lucky and it heals up well, which it is, that scar will reduce to nothing. But nothing like that has ever happened before, that fast, so don't get your hopes up."

"Okay. So, when can I leave?" Conner said.

"We're just going to run a few blood tests to try and see what makes you heal faster than others," the doctor explained.

"Oh I doubt you'll find out how he does that," Amelia said with a knowing smile.

"Do you know how he does that Doctor Heart?" the doctor asks, turning his attention toward her.

"No. I'm just guessing you won't find out."

"And why is that?" the doctor asked, looking offended.

"Don't look at me. It was just a hunch," Amelia told him, putting her hands up. Still looking offended the doctor held his walkie talkie to his ear because it had started saying something.

"They need you in the lobby, Doctor Heart," he told her. Amelia left, closing the door behind her softly.

"Sorry about that. We will figure it out. She's new here. I think she just started today," the doctor apologized.

"I think I know her from somewhere. Do you know what her job was before?" Jess questioned.

"Umm. . . I don't know," the doctor said.

"I've seen her before somewhere too," Jake added.

The twins shrugged. "I've never seen her," Conner told Jake.

"Her name's Amelia Heart right?" Izzy asked.

"Yes," the doctor looked at them suspiciously. He didn't like all the questions.

"So, how long will I be staying?" Conner asked, to try and distract the guy. Fortunately it worked. He went back to his clipboard.

"You'll be able to leave around nine a.m. tomorrow," he told Conner. "Would you like one of us to drive you home or do you have someone to drive you back?" the doctor asked.

"Umm. . . Could you?" Jake replied.

"Sure. I'll phone somebody. We need to do some tests on Conner. Would you like to wait in the lobby a little longer or go now?"

"We can go now," Jake offered after glancing at his siblings to make sure this was okay.

"Do you want to go with your mother or alone?"

"She's not our mother," Izzy said stiffly, "And we would like to go alone."

"Okay just a sec," the doctor started saying something in his walkie talkie, then saying to them "Go into the lobby and tell the woman working at the front desk that you are the ones who need a ride."

"Okay," Jess said, "Bye Conner."

"Bye Conner," Jake told his brother.

"Bye. Have fun!" Izzy told him.

"I'll try. Bye guys!"

They walked to the lobby and got a ride back home. It was around noon so after they got dropped off they took their bikes and went to Wendys. They biked back home and hid in their room. Jake locked the door so if Edel or Ms. Mafore came in, the siblings would have enough time to hide the food.

"So tomorrow are we going to go to the hospital on our bikes and bring Conner's?" asked Izzy.

"No he's going to be in a splint, remember?" Jake reminded her.

"We could ask the hospital workers to drop Conner off," Jess suggested.

"Sounds good. I think they already said that before anyway," Izzy agreed, taking a bite of her cheeseburger and adding, with her mouth full, "When have you two seen Amelia before?"

Jess answered, "I don't remember. It must have been a long time ago. But something about her just seems. . . I don't know. . . familiar. And off. Like kind of not entirely. . . I don't know. It just kind of seems weird. You know?"

"I've never met her, but what you said sorta, not really described what I was thinking," Izzy agreed, swallowing.

"That's how I feel too. I think we should do some research on her," Jake suggested.

"Okay. Jake, you're the only one with a computer. Can we use it?" Izzy asked.

"Sure," Jake answered, "But it's downstairs."

"We should probably just go down there anyway and get all of our things," Jess decided.

"Yeah. Should we bring the chest to make it easier?" Izzy asked.

"Probably," Jake agreed, taking out the chest.

They all walked downstairs to gather their things. Jess retrieved her phone from under the table just as it started ringing. She didn't recognize the number.

"Hello?" asked Jess.

"Hi. Am I speaking to either Jessica, Isabella, or Jake?" questioned the speaker.

"Maybe. Who are you?" challenged Jess, turning around and putting the phone on speaker so Izzy and Jake could hear.

"This is Doctor Miao, from the hospital. I spoke with you today in Conner's room."

"Is he all right?" inquired Izzy, sounding worried.

"Yes. Actually he's more than all right. He is completely healed and doesn't need a splint," he informed them.

"Really?" asked Jake, shocked.

"Yes. It's fantastic. Would you happen to know if anyone else in your family has this ability or any other special abilities?" Doctor Miao asked them eagerly. How could he have known? That wasn't a question most, or any, people would ask.

They exchanged worried glances. It seemed like a weird question. They didn't know how he could come up with it on his own. But still, should they tell him? Or did he actually know? Was he a bad guy? Or were they overthinking this? Why and how would he come up with that question? It didn't seem like a question a doctor or *anybody* would ask.

Jake gave a nervous laugh into the phone. "Not that we know of. I mean, our uncle can do some pretty weird things with balloons," Jake lied. The siblings knew nothing about their family.

"Oh. Well he's still going to stay overnight, just to be safe, but will you be able to pick him up in the morning?"

"Umm. . . Sure," replied Izzy.

"Okay. Well, bye now," the doctor hung up the phone.

"Should we bring his bike?" Izzy asked.

"Yeah. We need to get out for a while," confirmed Jake.

"How long is it to get to the hospital on our bikes?" said Jess.

"Umm. Probably around forty-five minutes to get there and another forty-five to get back," Jake said, doing some quick math.

"Ugh. An hour and a half. Seriously?" Jess wasn't on board with the idea.

"Yes. The fresh air will be good for us," prompted Jake.

"Okay. Fine," agreed Jess.

"I wonder how the heck Conner is healing up so fast," Izzy wondered out loud. Then she added, "Do you think we can all do that?"

"I'm not willing to stab myself with a piece of glass to find out," declared Jake.

"Neither am I," Jess argreed. They all helped each other carry the chest up the stairs.

"Shoot," sighed Jake when he saw their bedroom door open. They walked inside and saw all the walls had been scribbled on. Izzy muttered some choice words for Edel. The worst part: it was a permanent marker. Edel and Ms. Mafore must've gotten home while they were on the phone.

"Aww man," Izzy complained.

"Well can we do anything about it?" asked Jess.

"No. Unless Ms. Mafore has spare paint of this color. We could wait and use some of our money to buy a different color," suggested Jake. Their walls were a type of brown-green.

"Yeah. I hate this color," Jess agreed.

"It is pretty gross," Izzy added, discreetly taking some of Jess's fries.

"Okay. Well Edel actually did us a favor. I don't think any of us liked this color," said Jake.

Everybody was silent for a couple of minutes while they finished their food.

Then Jess yawned and said, "It's been a long day. I'm going to take a nap."

"Me too," Izzy agreed.

"Okay. Once we're done we can look up Amelia Heart," Jake laid down on his bed.

Jess and Izzy climbed the ladders to their bunks and almost immediately fell asleep. Jake lay awake a little longer thinking about his control over the weather. If this continued, and more people got hurt, he would have to find a way to stop it.

Chapter Four

Jake woke up first. Then he woke up Izzy and Jess.

"Uhhh. . . What time is it?" Izzy grumbled.

"Umm. . . Like two in the afternoon," replied Jake

"And what are we doing up?" asked Jess.

"We're going to research Amelia Heart, remember?" Jake reminded her.

"Oh right," said Jess.

"Get your laptop out Jake," instructed Izzy.

She took out her phone and Jess did the same. For a couple minutes there was silence.

"I can't find her," Izzy said eventually.

"Same. All the other Amelia Hearts in the world are popping up, but I can't find her," agreed Jess.

"Okay," Jake said, not having much luck either. "We should look at all the hospital staff."

They didn't know why they were obsessed with Amelia Heart, but they were. Jess looked up the Baystate Hospital staff. She scrolled through all the images and didn't find Amelia Heart.

"Huh that's weird," said Jess, confused.

"What?" said Izzy.

"She's not here," Jess told Izzy and Jake.

"Are you sure?" Jake asked.

"Yes. Maybe? I don't think so," said Jess.

"Let me see," demanded Izzy.

Jess showed Izzy her phone while Jake looked it up on his computer. Jake and Izzy checked and double checked each person. Then they used a search bar to look up her name on the front page. Nothing.

"Where the heck is she?" blurted Izzy after about an hour of this.

Jess shrugged. It wasn't very difficult to find an adult online. Or it shouldn't be. It was like Amelia Heart had just disappeared.

"Maybe she died?" suggested Izzy.

"Izzy!" scolded Jake.

"What? It was just an option," Izzy said defensively.

"We would have still seen her online. Besides she looked extremely healthy and well," argued Jake.

"Okay. Okay. I was just saying. It *could* have happened," insisted Izzy.

"Fine Izzy, she *could* have died," sighed Jake.

There was another couple minutes of silence, while they kept looking things up.

"So, you're all positive that you couldn't find *anything* on her? Not even the *tiniest* thing?" Jake asked hopefully.

"Nope. Not even the *tiniest* thing," Izzy answered.

"Are you sure? Was there something you missed?" Jake said.

"Jake. We are positively sure that we missed *nothing*?" Jess asked exasperated.

"Okay, okay," Jake said.

"Besides, instead of meeting Conner outside the hospital we can go inside and see her," Izzy told Jake.

"Yeah that seems like a good idea," Jake said.

By this time it was almost four. Jake called Conner and arranged to meet him in the lobby of the hospital. Jake didn't mention anything about Amelia. He would figure it all out tomorrow. They decided to get take-out. Izzy and Jess wanted sushi, but Jake wanted Chinese food.

Sushi won. Jess and Izzy were going to split a vegetarian roll while Jake had a spicy tuna roll, saving some for Conner. The delivery showed up around 5:45. They made sure that both the sushi and delivery guy stayed out of sight of Edel and Ms. Mafore.

They snuck the food upstairs and opened the packages. Izzy took out chopsticks while Jake and Jess went into the kitchen to get drinks and plates. They set it up on a little table and dug in. After eating, they all went on doing their separate things.

Jake was finishing an essay, Izzy was sketching on her bunk, and Jess was on the phone with one of her friends. Shortly after that they went to bed early. It had been a rough day and they were ready for it to be over.

The next morning they grabbed their bikes and Izzy attached Conner's to the back of hers with a little trailer. They rode for forty-five minutes in silence. Once they got to the hospital they found Conner in the lobby.

"Hey Conner. How ya feeling?" Izzy greeted him.

"Pretty good. Why did you guys want to meet in the lobby again?"

"We wanted to see Amelia Heart," Jake answered.

"Who's Amelia Heart?" asked Conner.

"You know that lady that was in your room before we came in?" Izzy asked him.

"Umm. . . I don't remember any lady there."

"You don't? She was shorter, had a big gray bun on top of her head, not a very great looking uniform. She was arguing with your doctor," Jess described.

"No. I've never seen her."

Was this a trick? Had Conner really never seen her? Did he just not remember her? "Well let's go to the front desk and try to find her," suggested Izzy slowly, staring at her brother.

They walked up to the front desk and asked the lady sitting there about Amelia Heart.

"Is she sick? What's her diagnosis?" the lady asked.

The siblings looked at each other.

"She uhh. . . she works here," Izzy told her.

"Umm, we have no Amelia Heart that works here," the lady responded, flipping through some papers.

All the siblings except Conner exchanged quizzical looks.

"Okay. . .? Then could we speak to Doctor Miao please?" Jess asked.

"Oh, Seb? Sure. One sec. I just have to make sure he's not with a patient or anything."

She took out her walkie talkie and said something into it.

"You're in luck, he's on break. He says he'll be right down," the lady told them.

The siblings walked away and sat down. A few moments later Doctor Miao walked in and talked to the lady at the front desk, who pointed at them.

"Hello there!" he greeted them.

"Hi Doctor Miao! We were just wondering about Amelia Heart? Is she still here?" Izzy asked him.

"Who?" the doctor asked, with a puzzled face.

"Amelia Heart? She was there when we came," Jess reminded the doctor.

"Uhh no. There was no one in the room except Conner, you three, and I."

"Yes there was. Don't you remember? You said you could probably figure out what was happening with Conner and she said she doubted it. Then you got all mad and she left the room" Jess reminded him.

"Umm, no. Are you thinking of a different person or time?"

"No. Do you really not remember?" Jake asked.

"Hang on. . ." Dr. Miao concentrated hard, and it looked as if he was on the edge of figuring something out. Then his face went blank. "Do you need to see somebody? Are you feeling okay?"

"We're *fine*. Conner, do you not remember this?" Izzy said.

"I don't," Conner answered, unsure, not knowing if they were okay.

"Oh yeah!" Doctor Miao said remembering something, "I forgot I wanted to test you guys out to see if you're anything like Conner."

The siblings had looked up when Doctor Miao had said that he remembered. Now they felt confused. "Umm. . . I think we would need time to think about it," Jake answered, startled with the quick change of subject.

The doctor looked at them with fascination. Did he know something about them?

"Well if there's nothing that you're keeping from me then you should be able to do it right?" Doctor Miao asked.

He was smart. He told them that if they don't complete the blood tests then he knew there was something up with them. And if they did do it he would probably find out how different they really are. Because it seemed like he did know that there was something unique about them.

"And another thing," he began and the siblings tensed, "We found out something different about Conner."

"What?" Jess asked.

"He doesn't have any of the known blood types in the world."

"I don't?" Conner asked.

"No."

"What are the known blood types again?" asked Jess.

"A-positive, A-negative, B-positive, B-negative, AB-positive, AB-negative, O-positive, O-negative, and I guess Rh-null," Jake recited.

"And Conner has none of those?" said Izzy.

"No," Doctor Miao replied.

"What kind of blood do I have then?" asked Conner.

"One that nobody has ever seen before."

"Well, is it bad?" Jake asked.

"I don't think it is necessarily bad, it's just that we've never heard or seen it before. Well, I mean I guess it might be bad, but it probably isn't," the doctor told them, with a slight chuckle.

"How can you tell if it's bad or not?" Izzy asked.

"It will show up at some point as a disease or something like that," Doctor Miao told them. "I want to test you to see if you have a different blood type than Conner. Or if you have the same. And also if you have the same "self-healing powers" as Conner. But we don't have to do this if you're not comfortable."

"Okay I guess," Jake said, exchanging glances with his siblings.

Doctor Miao led them to the elevator and took them up to floor five. He then took them down a hallway, took a right, then another right, and arrived at room number 508. He walked in and told them to take a seat on the beds. Conner and Izzy took one, while Jess and Jake took another.

The room was pretty small. A mini X-ray leaned on the wall along with a stethoscope which hung up above it on a hook. Shelves lined the walls with machines and tubes only doctors had. Two doctor beds were against a wall. The walls were pale, cream color and the ceilings were white.

The doctor took some equipment off the shelves and put them on a small table. Then he took the stethoscope and checked each of their heartbeats. Looking satisfied he hung it back up and turned back to them.

"Okay your heartbeats are fine," Doctor Miao said.

He grabbed a couple items off the table and headed towards the door. The siblings followed Doctor Miao out of the room and back to the elevator. He pressed the button to the 2nd floor. They walked out and down another hallway. Stopping at room number 227, Doctor Miao knocked to make sure no one was there. No one responded so he pushed the door open.

It was bigger than the last room. Inside there were a few machines attached to the wall. Lined up against the wall were two more beds. He gestured for them to sit. Like in the last room shelves lined one wall. There was a water cooler and trash bin in one corner.

Doctor Miao set his equipment on a desk and, taking one of the items, walked over to one of the machines attached to the wall. He turned it on and attached the cord he took from the desk to it. He proceeded to press all sorts of buttons and flipped a switch. The machine vibrated.

"Okay I'm going to take a little blood sample from each of you. It might pinch a little, but only for a second," the doctor explained.

He took out a needle and put something like sanitizer on their forearm. He then cleaned the needle with the same sanitizer. He took Jake's arm and flipped it over, so his forearm was showing.

Doctor Miao injected the needle into a vein and took it out. Jake flinched. The blood flowed from the needle to a tube and into a small vile.

"The needle is hollow so I can collect the blood. This is a new machine which can test blood without any mistakes," he explained, gesturing to the machine he had turned on.

He poured Jake's blood into a hole at the top of the machine.

"Red light means it's a blood type that's a different combination than we've seen, that something wrong happened, or that the blood type is different altogether. Green light means they are working on figuring out the blood type. Yellow light is A-negative, orange light is A-positive, blue light is B-negative, purple light is B-positive, black light is AB-negative, brown light is AB-positive, white light is O-negative, gray light is O-positive, and gold light is Rh-null," the doctor told them. The machine light turned green, and then flashed red.

"Okay so do I have the same blood type as Conner or not?" Jake asked.

"Umm, let me check."

"The doctor looked at the machine and turned it around, so a small electric screen

faced them. It said, "Blood type unidentified."
And under that a small string of numbers.

"No you don't," responded Doctor Miao.

"Then what kind of blood type does he have," questioned Conner.

"Another one we've never seen before," Doctor Miao sighed. "I just don't understand how this is possible. Nobody has ever seen either of these blood types before and we've discovered them both in the past days. I just don't understand." He sighed again.

"Well can you take Jess and I's blood types please?" asked Izzy.

"Sure. Just a sec."

He unhooked the needle from the tube and threw it into a small trash bin. He walked over to the machine and lifted a small cup out of it that held Jake's blood. He put a cap on it and tossed it into the trash. He walked over to a file cabinet and opened it. He grabbed a different needle and a small cup.

He placed the small cup into the hole of the machine. He then injected the needle into one of Izzy's veins as she looked away, grimacing. The blood collected into another small test tube and Doctor Miao put it into the hole of the machine. The machine started processing the blood and the light turned green.

Then it turned red. Doctor Miao groaned. "Don't tell me it's another new blood type," he muttered. Going over to check it he let out a sigh of relief. "It's the same as Jake's."

"Really? What about Jess's?" Jake asked.

"Hold on a sec."

The doctor threw away Izzy's blood and the needle. Then he took a new needle and cup from the cabinet. He dropped the new cup in the hole and hooked the needle up to the tube. He took out the old vile, replacing it with a new one.

He held the needle up to Jess and she nodded and looked away. He flipped over her wrist and stuck the needle into a vein. Jess winced. Blood flowed into the tube. The doctor pulled the needle away. The machine light turned green and then red.

Doctor Miao stared at the machine and slowly walked over to it. His face flooded with relief. "It's the same as Conner's."

"Okay. Now what?" Jess asked.

"Now we see if you have the same 'healing powers' as Conner," he said, putting air quotes around healing powers.

"So, how do we do that?" questioned Jake.

"We aren't going to have to stab ourselves with a piece of glass right?" Izzy asked, sounding worried.

"Umm. . . not exactly," the doctor told them, sounding nervous.

"Oh no. I am not stabbing myself with a piece of glass," Jess objected.

"You're not stabbing yourself with a piece of glass. But you *are* stabbing yourself."

"*What!?*" The siblings cried out in unison.

"It won't hurt," Doctor Miao assured them.

"I don't care if it doesn't hurt! We aren't stabbing ourselves! Do you even hear how crazy that sounds?" Jake said.

"What if we don't have the self-healing power that Conner does? We won't be able to do anything about it! We would just have to wait for it to heal on its own! And I am *not* waiting that long," protested Jess.

"Yeah. I have soccer and school to do," Izzy agreed.

"And I'm not letting my siblings get stabbed!" fumed Conner.

"Fine," Doctor Miao conceded. "But you need some fluids after the blood test. And I'll get you a band-aid."

"Fine," Jess agreed, still a bit suspicious.

He got some band-aids out of the cabinet and gave them to Jess, Izzy, and Jake. While they were putting them on Doctor Miao filled a cup with water. He turned around to add something to the water, but the siblings didn't notice.

He gave them each a cup and told them to lie down for a second. They obeyed and drank the "water." Each of them slowly drifted off as they drank, their thoughts getting slower, and not being able to comprehend what was happening. Doctor Miao was going to make them cooperate if they wanted to or not. He walked out of the room and down the hall, leaving the siblings unaware and unconscious.

Doctor Miao walked up a flight of stairs and into another room. This one was filled with gurneys. He stacked up four and requested help from a co-worker through his walkie talkie. He walked to the elevator with the gurneys and took them back to the room with the siblings.

He took one off the stack and lowered the gurney to the bed. He then rolled each of the siblings onto one and took them out into the hallway. Another man appeared and he helped Doctor Miao take them outside and to an ambulance.

The man left and Doctor Miao wheeled the helpless siblings into the ambulance.

Chapter Five

Doctor Miao and his assistants each plunged a big needle into Izzy, Jess, and Jake. Conner had already been tested and he had tested positive. Doctor Miao couldn't have another one like Conner. He just needed to find out if they had the same... *disorder* as Conner.

He twisted the needle deeper into Izzy's flesh. Right now the siblings wouldn't notice if there was a tornado around them, much less him and his assistants sticking needles into them. He didn't think they could feel anything. If they had the same disorder as Conner... no, he didn't want to think about it.

He swiftly pulled the needle out of her and saw blood flow from the tube into a bottle. His assistants, following his lead, did the same. "You are not needed anymore," he said to the assistants who left the room. Doctor Miao did several tests on the blood, seeing if it had the same blood cells as Conner.

It would take a couple of days to come in, but he should see the results in the children soon. He only had to keep them in this room without anybody noticing overnight. The serum he had used would wear off in a couple hours and he didn't have any more at the hospital.

He would have to chain them down somehow. He knew there were some beds downstairs that could clip you down. He just had to make sure nobody came in here while he was downstairs. Doctor Miao put a sign on the door that said, "Surgery in progress, please do not disturb." He took the elevator downstairs and grabbed two beds out of a room.

He took them back upstairs and strapped Conner and Izzy into them. He got two more beds from downstairs and strapped up Jess and Jake. He started to do more tests on their blood, skin, and overall DNA.

Chapter Six

The siblings had gone into a deep sleep sometime during all the testing and were now waking up, five hours later. Izzy groggily opened her eyes. Her mind felt super fuzzy. It was the same with Conner, Jess, and Jake. "What happened?" asked Conner.

They searched their minds, struggling to remember. Jake gasped as it came back to him. "Doctor Miao kidnapped us! He must have *really* wanted to do those experiments! I'm guessing he wants to continue them on us, so that's why we're strapped in," Jake said.

"Do you think we can get out?" Jess wondered, already struggling and jerking her body back and forth.

"I'm afraid that's quite impossible." The siblings strained and looked around. Doctor Miao came out of the shadows holding a clipboard and eating a salad. The siblings were starving. They hadn't had anything to eat since yesterday morning.

Wait. Was it a new day? It seemed like it, but there was no way of telling. How long had they been asleep? How long had Doctor Miao done tests on them? As if he heard their thoughts he said, "It's two in the morning of May twentieth. I've had plenty of time to do tests on your blood and DNA." They had been asleep for *five hours.*

"You wouldn't be able to get us any food would you?" Conner asked sarcastically.

"I can't mess up the tests. So far I'm pretty sure you don't have the same. . . *disorder* as Conner here."

"You tested us to see if we had the same *self-healing powers* as Conner? What did you *do*!?" Izzy yelled.

"Calm yourself. I didn't mean any harm. I just wanted to test you. I stuck a needle and made an incision in your legs. Well, except for Conner."

Jess, Izzy, and Jake all looked down at their legs while Conner stared in disgust at the doctor. There was a long, but shallow cut in their legs. Dried blood surrounded it. "So you cut them open and now you're just going to leave them like this?" Conner asked in disgust.

"I could stitch it if you want?" Doctor Miao offered cheerfully.

"And have you come near me again? No thanks," Izzy snapped.

"Children, I'm sorry. I wanted to see why you have these traits in you." He sounded sincere, but he had lost every bit of the siblings' trust. He kept changing personalities within seconds.

"There are other ways to do that besides locking us up and sticking knives into us," Jess said.

"I had to see if you had the same self-healing, well I guess you would call it a gene, as Conner. And. . . also something else."

"Well now you can see that we don't and where does that put us? We have huge scars on our legs that's going to take a pretty long time to heal on their own! And on top of that we were kidnapped by an evil scientist!" Jake yelled.

Then they realized they were still in the hospital. "Okay guys on the count of three scream as loud as you can. We want people to hear us." Jake told them.

"One. Two. *Three!*"

They all started yelling as loud as their vocal cords would allow them to. The doctor didn't even make a move to stop them. He let them scream until they were out of air and their throats were raw. "So sorry children, but the walls are soundproof." He sounded like he really meant it.

"You vile imbecile. Why would you do this to innocent children?" Izzy asked. "You—"

"Well I would hardly call you innocent. Do you guys remember this?" he asked while gesturing toward a TV screen. The screen showed a huge tornado at the soccer field. The camera zoomed in on Jake. His eyes were yellow.

"Correct me if I'm mistaken, but your eyes aren't yellow are they? I'm pretty sure all of you have blue eyes," Doctor Miao asked Jake.

The siblings stayed silent. "And," he added, "I am positive that you created this tornado. So, you lied when I asked you about other "powers" you had. You also conjured this tornado, which could have hurt more people, but didn't. It hurt your brother Conner and he had to come here, which is when I saw his disorder. That caused me to test on you. So, this is all actually *Jake's* fault."

"*Don't you dare try to blame Jake! You* were the one who started *experimenting* on us. WITHOUT OUR PERMISSION," Jess fumed.

"Oh well children. Your tests are almost over. Then I'll get you something to eat. Once you're done, since I can't have people knowing about me doing this, I'm going to use a special injection that I created and use it on you."

"What does it do?" Izzy asked, her voice low. Part, well most of her actually, didn't want to know.

"It. . . well. . . it will make you insane. You will not remember anything about yourself or anybody else. You won't know how to speak. You will be a pointless human being. This creation works by attacking your brain cells, memories, and personalities that make you, you. It will destroy them, rendering you worthless. Do know that I am very, *very* sorry about this, and remember, all of this could have been avoided had you just let me do the experiments when I wanted to. But as I can't have people like you running around, at least not here, and you seem very different from the others I know, you may not be allowed to get away unharmed." And with that, he left the room.

"Well this is bad," Izzy said.

"Ya think? Jake, do you think you can, like, summon wind or something and get us out of here," Conner said.

"Umm. . . how?"

"You can bring the wind in here and have it blow so hard that it snapps the cuffs on us," Conner explained.

"I guess I can try. Do you really think he invented that injection?"

"Unfortunately, yes. He seemed to know a lot about it and what it does," Izzy said, sounding anxious. The tough facade she had put up in front of Dr. Miao was fading.

"It doesn't matter. He won't have a chance to test it if *you just open up these cuffs*," Jess said.

"Right," Jake said.

He went into a state of deep concentration. The twins felt the wind blow near them. Suddenly the cuffs released off of them and they fell forward. Barely managing to catch themselves, they ran out of the room. Unexpectedly Izzy shoved them into a different room when they were halfway through the building.

"Get in, get *in*," she hissed. She quietly closed the door behind them.

"What the heck Izzy?" Conner said.

"Shush! Doctor Miao was walking down the hall," Izzy whispered.

"Really? How do you know?" Jess said, looking out of the door's window. Izzy yanked her back, and they both toppled over.

"Yes. Just wait a sec. Then we can go," Izzy said, crouching and dusting herself off.

She looked out of the window. "Okay. The coast is clear." She opened the door and started sprinting up the hall. They made it outside to where their bikes were parked. They hopped on and sped off. They were silent the whole ride home. They quickly threw their bikes in the garage and ran up to their room. They sat down gasping for breath.

"That *maniac*," Izzy said after a while.

"Yeah. He's terrible," Conner agreed. That was an understatement.

"*He messed up my look*," Jess said.

"Who cares? There is an insane, possible criminal, who wants to cut us up!" Jake said.

"Yeah *that's what I'm talking about*! He messed up my leg, ruining my *whole look*," Jess said.

"Speaking of that, we should probably wash and bandage these," Izzy suggested.

They all walked up into the small, cramped bathroom and sat on the edge of the bathtub. Jake turned on the hot water. The tub filled about halfway before he shut it off. They each took turns with the soap and cleaned out their cuts, meanwhile Conner was in their room searching for Doctor Miao on the internet.

Once they were done they walked back into their room and asked Conner how he was doing. "Terrible," he said, "It's so weird, I can't find any mention of Doctor Miao anywhere!"

"Really? It was the same with Amelia, we could never find her," Jess said.

"Guys? There was never any Amelia! I don't know why you keep saying there was," Conner said.

"Yes there was Conner! I don't know what that doctor did to you and if you had some brain damage done, but there was an Amelia Heart!" Jake said.

"Guys, are you sure that we actually saw an Amelia Heart? I mean, the doctor did stuff to you too!" Conner argued.

"Wait! Ms. Mafore saw her! Let's just go ask her," Jess said.

They all ran to the kitchen where Ms. Mafore was chopping veggies. "Umm, Ms. Mafore?" Izzy asked, "Do you know who Amelia Heart is?"

Ms. Mafore flinched. "I have no idea who you're talking about."

"Really? She told you that you weren't allowed to see Conner and then you got mad and stomped off?" Izzy said, hopping from foot to foot.

"I have never heard or seen such a woman," Ms. Mafore said stiffly. She wasn't very convincing.

"Are you sure? She came up to you right as you were about to see Conner. She was shorter, with a big gray bun on the top of her head? You really don't remember her?" Izzy asked.

"No. And as you can see I'm busy. Leave. *Now.*"

The siblings rushed back up to their room. "I told you. Ms. Mafore has no idea who Amelia Heart is," Conner said.

"Conner, it was obvious that Ms. Mafore was lying." Jake pointed out.

"Yeah and did you see her flinch when Izzy mentioned her name?" Jess said.

"She was definitely hiding something," Izzy agreed.

"Yeah I guess," Conner said, looking stumped. Who *was* Amelia Heart?

"What are we going to tell the school about why we weren't there today?" Jess said.

"It's fine. The school was closed anyway. I got an email about it," Jake said.

"Why?" Izzy asked.

"The tornado did a ton of damage," Jake said looking down.

"Oh, Jake. the tornado wasn't your fault," Izzy said, putting her hand on her brother's shoulder.

"Yeah, okay," Jake said, not convinced.

"Well at least we won't have to make up any work," Conner said, trying to change the subject.

"Yeah I guess," Jake said.

"Well we can keep talking about this later, but right now I have an essay to finish," Izzy said.

"Oh yeah I forgot about that," Conner said, going to get his backpack.

They started working on that together, while Jess talked on her phone with her boyfriend explaining why she couldn't meet him today, and Jake started researching about controlling the weather and self-healing. "It says here that every time somebody claims they have control over the weather, it's just them pretending they can," Jake said, disappointed.

"Just for the record Jake I don't think you're pretending," Izzy said playfully, looking up from her essay.

"Me either," Conner said.

Jess made motions for them to be quiet. Izzy rolled her eyes and went back to her essay. Conner and Izzy had to be hushed by Jess a lot because they were working together out loud. Every once in a while Jake would say what he found on the internet and Jess would "shh" him too. It was pretty peaceful for a while.

Then Ms. Mafore came in. "Dinner's ready," she snapped. They got up and walked into the kitchen. What they saw surprised them. Laid out on the table was chicken and salad for *everybody*. Not just Ms. Mafore and Edel, but the siblings too. In their whole life of living here they had almost never had an actual meal that was the same as Ms. Mafore and Edel.

"Umm, where's ours?" Conner asked, confused.

"Don't be silly, this is yours," Ms. Mafore said stiffly.

"It is? Why? Is it over the due date?" Jess asked suspiciously.

"No. I thought that we could have a nice dinner," she said, her tone suggesting that she did not at all want that.

"Umm okay?" Conner said and sat down.

Everybody stayed silent the whole time. The siblings thought that this was the best meal they had eaten in a long time. They didn't even get the bad parts of the chicken.

"Just so you know the inspector is coming over in two days and I want all of you to be on your best behavior. I need you to clean the bathroom, kitchen, all of the bedrooms, the basement, and the living room."

The siblings' mouths dropped open. Never in all their years of living had they had to clean *anything*. They had to clean up their room every once in a while. But today was the first day in a year that they've had to clean *their room*. And now Ms. Mafore was asking them to clean the *whole house*. "Oh and you have to clean the floors, windows, and walls. Somebody will be bringing in a new window which you will have to insert."

They just sat there. "What about Edel?" Jess asked indignantly.

"What about her?" Ms. Mafore said.

"Will she have to clean or anything?" Jake said.

"She will supervise."

Edel smirked at them. Then Ms. Mafore added, "She will tell you if you have done enough and if you need to clean more. She will decide which of you clean what. She's going to tell you how to rearrange your room.

Right now it's terrible to look at. She will tell you how to rearrange her playroom downstairs. Actually you can leave my room as it is. Oh and you also have to do yard work."

The siblings made noises of outrage. Edel was positively beaming with delight.

"Mommy?" she said, "I saw that they had drawn on their walls. Can I make them get a new paint color?"

"Yes. I have some money set aside for re-doing rooms."

"Okay. Can I make them get new furniture?"

"Yes. You may do whatever you want as long as it's in the budget."

"Oh no. Sorry, but we can't do any of that. We have school tomorrow," Conner said, and his siblings looked relieved.

"Did you four not get the emails from the school? You have the next two weeks off.

The tornado damaged the school," she said, looking smugly at them.

"No! I got an email saying that the school had only closed for today!" Jake said.

"Yes. You may want to recheck your email. There was a lot more damage done than originally thought."

"And what if we don't want to do this? What if we tell the inspector what a horrible woman you are?" Izzy said.

"Then I will take you to the hospital to see Doctor Miao again," she replied.

"You wouldn't! Wait, how did you know about that?" Jess asked.

"Well I didn't know for sure until you told me, but I had a suspicion about why you were home so late."

Jake threw a look that said "Stop talking!" at Jess.

"Fine we'll do it, but we expect none of our belongings to be touched," Jake said, trying to look as intimidating as possible.

"Well I won't promise that. It's Edel who will decide what goes in your room and what doesn't."

"Well then at least give us time to go and prepare," Jake said, now looking desperate.

"Fine. You have ten minutes before bed."

"Ten minutes! It's only like six thirty!" Izzy said.

"Yes, but you have a long day ahead of you. Clock starts now," Ms. Mafore said, smirking.

Without clearing their plates, the siblings ran to their room. "That evil woman!" Izzy hissed. "Her and Dr. Miao deserve each other."

"Well there's nothing we can do now, so we might as well just get on with it," Jake said.

"I don't *want* to do it! Why can't we just run away or something?" Izzy asked.

"I'd loved to Iz. But where would we run?" Jake said.

"I don't know! Somewhere that's not here! Someplace where we don't have to worry about evil orphan ladies and psycho doctors!" she snapped.

"Izzy calm down. We're not going anywhere. The police would track us down. And what about school, soccer, and our friends," Conner said gently. She took a couple deep breaths.

"We better start hiding things. We only have five minutes," Jess said, checking her phone.

"Okay. I guess. What do you think Edel is going to do with our room?" Izzy asked.

Jake shrugged and started gathering his things. It was silent for a while. They stowed away almost everything that was in their room.

Then Ms. Mafore came in just as Izzy was putting the carpet back. Her eyes lingered on her for a moment and said curtly, "Bed." Then she walked out of the room.

Conner turned the lights off and Jake got out some flashlights. They kept on hiding their items and getting everything ready. By the time they actually went to bed it was almost midnight. The next day was basically torture for the siblings. Jess had to do the yardwork, Izzy had to install the new window, Conner had to clean the bathrooms, and Jake had to redo Edel's room.

They all finished around the same time and took a thirty minute lunch break. Jake started making sandwiches, while Izzy and Conner got out drinks and plates. Izzy went into a fit of giggles as Jess came in through the back door. "What happened to you?" Conner asked, laughing. She looked terrible. Grass stains covered her jeans and blouse, which was white. Bad choice.

Her hair was all messed up and had twigs and bits of grass sticking out of it. Dirt was smeared all over her face. Mud covered her shoes. Grass covered her head to toe. "Two racoons happened to me. One was normal and one was Edel. The first one chased me through a bunch of bushes and into a mud puddle and it got splattered everywhere. Edel dumped all of my lawnmower clippings on me when I was done. Then she had a huge bucket of mud which she then *also* dumped on me," she snarled.

"Well we're on lunch break for about thirty minutes so I guess you can take a quick shower," Jake said, starting to laugh.

"Fine," she snapped and stomped up the hall.

"Hey, wait! I just cleaned that!" Conner said.

"Oh well. I guess you'll have to clean it again," Izzy said, giggling as she started eating.

Conner grumbled as they took their sandwiches from the plate. Edel walked in the kitchen, looking smug. She took the last sandwich (which was supposed to be Jess's) off the plate. "Edel, that's Jess's," Izzy said. Edel spit on part of the bread.

"Never mind," Izzy said, turning away.

"So," Edel began, "I need all of you to help me with redoing your room, because it needs a lot of work. Where's Jess?"

"In the shower washing off the grass and mud that *you* dumped on her," Izzy said, rolling her eyes.

Edel just shrugged and told them, "Mommy is out buying new furniture and paint that I picked out for your room." Then she walked out of the room.

"That *little brat*," Izzy muttered under her breath.

"She'll get what's coming to her someday," Conner said, shrugging.

"I sure hope so," Izzy said, sighing.

"Anyway, how bad do you think Edel's going to mess up our room, on a scale of one to ten?" Conner asked.

"About a million," Jake said, miserably.

"Do you think we'll be able to change it back after?" Izzy said.

"No way. It'll be messed up way too much," Conner said.

They ate in silence until Jess came down. "Where's mine?" she demanded.

"In Edel's stomach," Izzy replied.

"Oh well. I'll just have the leftover sushi," Jess said.

"You guys got sushi! How did you afford that?" Conner asked.

Izzy checked that neither Ms. Mafore or Edel was there. "From Ms. Mafore's wallet. Like everything else," she whispered.

Jess opened the refrigerator and pulled out the hidden compartment that Jake installed so they could keep their food hidden without Ms. Mafore or Edel knowing. She took out the sushi and chopsticks and started eating.

She had just finished when Ms. Mafore came back. "Take this to your room," she said, dropping some paint cans on the ground for the siblings to pick up. They quickly finished their lunches and brought the paint upstairs, where they saw Edel waiting. "Okay Edel, what are we going to have to do?" Izzy said wearily.

"Well you need to paint, which means you have to move all of your stuff. Then you have to only keep your beds in here, while I tell you where things are going to go," she replied.

Conner groaned and started moving out everything but the beds. Izzy helped him while Jake and Jess moved their beds to the middle of the room. They each grabbed a paint brush and started painting with the color Edel had chosen for them. It was an off-white color, so it wasn't that bad.

It took them the rest of the day to finish painting and then they had to sleep in there while the paint dried. If you have ever been in a room that has been freshly painted it smells *terrible*. The next day they were up at around four, moving all the new furniture into their room. At around seven Edel came in and told them, "Hurry up and eat."

They ate a fast breakfast and walked back upstairs. "Okay," Edel ordered, "I'm going to put the finishing touches on the wall and you four can start arranging the furniture the way I drew it on the paper." She gave them a crumpled up piece of paper. "I convinced Mommy you don't have to clean the basement so you can have more time to redo your room. You're welcome."

Izzy uncrumpled the paper. It showed a bad sketch of their room with a bunch of blobs in it. "*How* are we supposed to know what these things are?" she asked.

"I don't know how you can't read that. I know my drawings are a *lot* better than yours, so it might take time for you to figure out what *true art* looks like," Edel said with an air of superiority.

"Why you little. . .," Izzy growled. She was *very* proud of her drawings, and most of them were quite good. Jake and Conner had to grab her arms to stop her from lunging at Edel.

"Little what? Don't be swearing in front of *me*. I'll run and tell Mommy. Now get to work," Edel commanded them. Ms. Mafore had made a very strict no-swearing policy. Izzy was the only one who had trouble following it.

Conner whispered something in his twin's ear and calmed her down. Conner whispered the same thing to Jess and Jake when Edel's back was turned. He was telling them they could arrange their room however they wanted, because Edel wouldn't know the difference. Izzy grinned and grabbed a desk, starting to set it up.

The furniture that Edel had bought wasn't that bad. Except for a Hello Kitty chair and My Little Pony sheets, most of the stuff was something you would normally find in a bedroom. When they were done they each had a small desk and there was a coffee table in the middle of the room with a fluffy carpet under it.

None of them were paying attention to what Edel was doing until she stepped back and said, "Done," with a couple markers in her hand. On their walls were badly drawn flowers, unicorns, Hello Kitty characters, and mermaids. "Oh. My. God," Izzy breathed, "That's it. I'm going to kill that kid." Then she lunged at Edel. Jake and Conner barely grabbed her in time. Jess had to help them because Izzy was struggling so much.

Edel, thinking smartly, ran out of their room and locked the door behind her. Then something weird happened. Izzy slipped through their fingers and *transformed into a bee*. Jess shrieked and started swatting at the bee. Conner fell backwards in shock while Jake just stood there, stunned. The bee flew through their open door and got through the crack in Edel's room. Soon screams filled the house.

The siblings heard Ms. Mafore running up the stairs, but none of them moved. "Edel!? EDEL!? Open the door! It's locked! EDEL OPEN THE DOOR AND MOMMY WILL HELP YOU!" she screamed.

Edel's wailing continued and Ms. Mafore kept banging on the door. A bee flew through the crack in the door and landed on the siblings bed. It transformed back into Izzy and she lay on Conner's bed with her eyes closed. Conner ran over followed quickly by Jake and Jess.

"Izzy?" Conner said, shaking her. "Izzy wake up!"

Her eyes flew open and she gasped. She looked exhausted. "Oh God. Oh God. Oh God!" she muttered.

"Izzy, are you okay? What just happened? Are you okay?" Conner repeated.

"I'm fine, just tired," she muttered and closed her eyes again.

"Izzy?" Conner said again. "Stay awake. What. Just. Happened?"

"Don't know. Felt tinier. Kept poking Edel. Hard. Went through the crack in the door," she said and promptly fell asleep.

"Oh my God," Conner said, "Is she okay?"

"I think," Jake said, checking her pulse. "She's just sleeping."

"Jake, what the heck just happened?," Conner asked.

Chapter Seven

Izzy woke up seeing her siblings' worried faces hovering over her. "Umm guys? Why are you doing that?"

"Izzy, are you okay?" Jess asked, looking worried.

"Yeah? Why are you guys acting so weird? Did something happen?" Then she gasped. "Oh my God! I transformed! That was so cool! It felt so good! I stung Edel! Oh my God! I have powers like Jake and Conner! Oh my *GOD!*"

"You sure you feel okay?" Conner asked. "You like, passed out once you got back in here. You weren't speaking in full sentences and you couldn't even keep your eyes open."

"Well, I think I'm fine." She got up from Conner's bed. "Yep. I'm fine. Do you think I can do that again?"

"I doubt you have control over it. I mean Jake doesn't. It's just whenever he gets mad. And, believe me, you were *super* mad," Conner said.

"Well he got the tornado under control eventually," Izzy said, closing her eyes.

She stood like that for a couple minutes.

"Did it work?" she asked, opening her eyes.

"Nope," Conner. He added, "I think it only happens when you can't control your emotions."

"Does this mean that Jess is going to get some powers too?" Izzy wondered.

"I don't know. Maybe," Jake said.

"I hope I do. What do you think it could be?" asked Jess.

"Hmm. . . I don't know. Let's look it up," Jake said, walking to his new desk to get his chromebook. They crowded around him as he looked up different powers. "That's cool. I'd like to have invisibility," Jess said, pointing to it.

"Yeah I think I would like invisibility," Conner said.

"I prefer shapeshifting," Izzy said, shrugging, "Wait, do you think I can transform into humans? What if I could transform into one of you?"

"If you could do that to your control you would probably get us into tons of trouble," Conner said.

"You know me so well," Izzy said, grinning as she nudged her twin.

"What if I could, like, read people's minds? That would be so amazing. Then I could find out if they like my outfit, and I could tell everybody my enemies' secrets!" Jess said.

"Well if you can do that at some point, I want my privacy," Izzy said.

"Okay, but it'll cost ya," Jess said, teasing her.

"How much?" Izzy asked.

"Uh. . . a hundred bucks! You have to pay up front," Jess answered.

"A hundred dollars! No way! Nice try Jess," Izzy said.

"Oh, I meant a hundred bucks a *day*."

"Well I wouldn't pay you either way," Izzy said.

"Okay," Jess smiled. "It'll be free for my family."

"Yeah. Spy on anyone else you want! Just not us," Conner said.

"Guys," Jess said, suddenly serious, "What are we going to do about this? I mean, Jake can control the weather, Conner can heal himself, and Izzy can turn into a bee. We have an evil doctor chasing after us, wanting to cut us up, and a rude orphanage lady with an awful daughter taking care of us. What if your powers escalate and you can't break out of the trance they put you in? What would happen then?"

"We would deal with it," Jake said, putting his arm around Jess, "We would help each other out of the trances and make sure Doctor Miao and his assistants don't find us. We would learn how to control our powers. And I'm going to be out of here in two years anyway."

"But you don't have enough money to rent an apartment and we couldn't come with you to college," Jess said.

Jake shrugged. "I could sneak you guys into my dorm."

"That would be fun," Izzy said, smiling. "And we wouldn't have to go to school! We could just chill in his dorm all day."

"Yeah, I don't know how that's gonna work," Conner said. "How are we going to sneak into a college and live there without anyone noticing?"

"Moving on. How are we going to learn how to control our powers?" Jake asked.

"Umm. . . well. . . we just don't get angry?" Izzy suggested.

"And how are we supposed to do that? Ms. Mafore and Edel make us angry all the time and so do some of the kids at school," Jess pointed out.

"School counselors?" suggested Conner.

"No. Way," Jess said, "I would never let myself be seen with such people."

"Jess? You're going to have to see the school counselors at some point to discuss your college opportunities," Jake said.

"Well I don't want to see the anger management school counselors," declared Jess.

"Yeah, me either," admitted Izzy.

"I don't really want to either," said Conner.

Jake shrugged. He didn't really want to either, although he knew they helped a lot of kids. They all thought about what they could do to stop getting angry. "Yoga and meditation?" Izzy said, half joking.

"I guess. But I don't know how that will help solve our problem. I've never tried yoga or meditation," Jake said.

Jess shrugged, "I'm okay with it. I mean, it's better than going to the school counselors. No offense to them or anything. I just don't think we need that."

"Yeah. I don't know. How will yoga help? It's not like we have anger management issues or anything. We just get angry like any normal person. It's just our temper tantrums that aren't normal," Conner said.

"Yup," Izzy agreed, "I don't really see how yoga will help either."

"But Iz, you were the one who suggested it," Jess said.

"I know. I just don't think it's that good of an idea anymore."

Jake shrugged and said, "Maybe we can just try and get our anger under control. We don't usually get angry much, we've just had some stressful weeks."

"Yeah. Do you think there's some superpower school that we could go to? And they could train us and we could be heroes and save lives?" Jess laughed.

"I wish. We could wear superhero masks and be super secret," Izzy giggled.

"Yeah. I would be the leader and you all would be my sidekicks," Conner said, in a kingly tone.

"You wish," Izzy said, giving her brother a playful shove.

"Yup, I do wish," Conner said, pushing her back.

They kept on joking and laughing for a while, enjoying one of the rare moments when they got to. Eventually Ms. Mafore called them in for dinner. And for the second time in their lives, they had a real dinner. They silently wondered how long this would go on for. "So, Ms. Mafore, when's the inspector coming tomorrow?"

"At around noon, and I expect you four to be on your best behavior."

"What about me mommy?" Edel asked.

"You're always on your best behavior, sweetheart."

"They aren't, right?" Edel said, pointing to the siblings.

"No. They have horrible manners and terrible posture."

Edel looked satisfied and the siblings looked bored. They were used to this. They went through it every day. It was the same thing again and again. Edel tried to humiliate them or get them in trouble every single day of their lives. What's new? The siblings cleared their plates and went to their room.

"So," Izzy said, flopping down on Conner's bed, "What are we going to tell the inspector?"

"What do you mean," Jake asked.

"What are we going to tell him about Ms. Mafore and Edel and this terrible house?" she asked, gesturing to the walls.

"Nothing. You heard what she said. She's going to hand us over to Doctor Miao if we say anything," Jess said, sitting down on a cushion near the coffee table.

"How? We can tell the inspector everything, including the threats, and then we'll be gone before she can even call Doctor Miao."

"And if she tracks us down?" Jake said.

"Umm. . . we can get fake IDs. And we can change our names? I dunno."

"Izzy, this place is better than the hospital. We don't want to go back there again. Besides, how are we going to hide three kids with special powers?" Conner said sitting on one of the pillows near her.

Izzy shrugged, looking defeated. "I just want to get away from here," she whispered.

"Yeah I know. We all do Iz, just wait. The time *will* come," Jake said, putting his arm around her and Conner.

"Yeah I guess," Izzy said, wrapping her hands around her knees tightly.

Chapter Eight

The next day the inspector came over. She was very sweet and friendly to the siblings. She gave them candy and said she hoped they were having a good time. They lied and said it was awesome there. She left saying that the house was in "tip top shape!" The siblings retreated to their bedroom and started unwrapping some of their candy. Jess bit into Almond Joy while Izzy shoved two Milky Ways into her mouth.

Jake and Conner shared a pack of Twinkies. They spent the whole day in their room, researching anything that had to do with special magic or kids having superpowers. They skipped lunch and were starving by dinner time. When they walked into the dining room they discovered that they were back to the horrible dinners. The siblings had some stale crackers and moldy cheese.

Edel and her mother had Wendy's. Instead of the usual rude remarks about the siblings at dinner, Edel looked like she was thinking about something very deeply. "Mommy?" she asked, her mouth full of vanilla frosty.

"Yes, honey?"

"I was wondering if we could get a doggie?"

Ms. Mafore looked like she was actually contemplating the situation. "What kind of doggie?" she asked carefully.

"A yellow one," Edel said, trying to look as innocent and cute as possible.

"I would, but I don't think we have enough money."

The siblings were stunned she was even considering it. When Izzy was smaller, around six, she had asked for a dog. Ms. Mafore had turned her down before she had even finished the question. But of course, she would do anything for Edel.

"What if we got one from the shelter?" She was not going to give up.

"If it's cheap enough, I guess. I can take you to the shelter tomorrow if you'd like that, sweetie."

"Yes! I would love that! Can we get a girl? Can I name her?"

"Sure."

That night the siblings all sat around the coffee table talking about a dog.

"I would love to have a pet!" Izzy squealed.

"Yeah. What do you think Edel's going to name it?" Conner said.

"EJ. Edel junior," Jess said seriously.

"Yeah. What if she gives it a really terrible name? I already feel bad for the poor dog," Jake said.

"Yeah, but if she does end up getting a dog, we would take care of it right?" Izzy said, hopefully.

"Yeah probably," Conner said, though he sounded excited about it.

The next day Edel and her mother really did go to a dog shelter. The siblings went too. But that was only so they could watch Edel while Ms. Mafore went shopping. Izzy got pretty attached to a dirty, golden retriever puppy. She spent the whole time with him and so did Edel. Izzy mostly tried to keep Edel from torturing the poor puppy, though she didn't really have to. Anytime Edel came near the dog it just ran behind Izzy.

When Ms. Mafore came back, Edel told her she wanted the golden retriever. The siblings stared open-mouthed and shocked as Ms. Mafore walked up to the counter to buy the dog. Edel scooped up the puppy, who started whimpering, and walked out the door with it.

"Come on," Ms. Mafore hissed.

The siblings ran out the door after them. The puppy was squirming and whining as Edel struggled to keep a hold on it. Ms. Mafore unlocked the car and Edel got in the front, forcing all the siblings to squish in back. Even a bigger car is only meant for three people in the back. Ms. Mafore had a tiny car. Each was made into a sandwich, their arms squeezed at their sides. Izzy was pushed onto Jess's lap, and nobody was wearing a seatbelt.

Over the next few days nothing interesting happened. Edel spent most of her time trying to find her puppy, who she named Otis. Weirdly, Otis always seemed to be in the siblings' room. He only listened to Izzy and always followed her around.

Izzy loved him and the two got along super well. Without any training at all, he obeyed her even if the command was really ridiculous. He would even do a backflip if she asked. Somehow she knew that nothing she asked him to do would harm the dog. Otis also liked Jess, Jake, and Conner, just not as much as Izzy. They didn't mind. They just liked seeing Izzy happy with Edel's puppy.

There were many tantrums on Edel's side. She hated that her puppy paid more attention to the siblings than he did to her. But, Edel wouldn't give up on Otis. Most of the time she locked him in her room with her, but somehow, almost like magic, he always ended up in the siblings room. But that wasn't the most interesting part of the week.

It happened on the siblings' first day back at school. At lunch break Izzy and Conner were playing soccer, Jake was in a Science Club meeting inside the school, and Jess was chatting with some of her friends. Izzy had just scored a goal with Conner's help and the other team wasn't being very nice about it. They really didn't seem to like that one of the only girls on the team had just scored on them.

Instead of bringing the ball to the middle like they were supposed to, the other team just started at their end. Thomas dribbled the ball up and his teammates ran on all sides of him. Whenever anyone from the opposing team came near them Thomas's bodyguards pushed them down. "Hey! FOUL!" Izzy yelled.

She ran towards them and wove in between, stealing the ball. Thomas ran after her and pushed her hard from behind. She fell, but absorbed its impact with a roll over. "What the heck, Thomas!?" she yelled. Conner ran over to help, she was already back up on her feet, and super mad.

They ran after Thomas together. Izzy stole the ball again and passed it to Conner. He fired a shot from half field and scored. They high-fived right before Thomas came over and ruined it. He ran over, spinning Izzy around from her shoulder and then punching her in the jaw. She stumbled and fell, but wasn't hurt badly. Thomas actually wasn't that strong. Izzy muttered some very colorful words as she tried to lunge at Thomas, but somebody had already gotten there.

Some invisible force knocked him to the ground and he tightened himself into a ball as something began kicking him. Thump, thump, thump. He whimpered and Izzy backed away. Then the noises stopped and Thomas got up. Izzy brought her arm back and punched him in the face. Thomas fell to the ground again, groaning. Suddenly Conner appeared behind Izzy, looking confused.

Thomas ran away just as a lunch monitor came over. "What is going on here?" she demanded.

"Nothing," Izzy muttered. "Come on Conner." She tugged on his arm and they ran away from the scene.

"What did you just do?" Izzy asked him in awe, once they were far enough away from the soccer.

"What do you mean? I just pushed Thomas from behind and kicked him a couple times, didn't I?"

Just then the bell rang. "Once school is over, we *have* to talk. Since it's the beginning of summer and super hot out, I'll talk to Jake and Jess about getting ice cream after school, okay?" Izzy asked him.

"Sure," Conner said, and together they ran back to school.

After school the four siblings walked to Coach's Ice Cream Shop together. "So why did you ask to come here, Iz?" Jess asked.

"Well, today at lunch break, Conner and I were outside playing soccer. It's Friday, so everybody was waiting to get out of school and were getting super hyped up. I scored and Thomas was being a jerk, he hit me."

"Really? Are you okay? Do you want me to do something about it?" Jake asked.

"I'm fine, but that's not the point. And you don't have to, Conner already did."

"What did you do Conner?" Jess asked him.

"Nothing! I just pushed him from behind and kicked him a couple times!"

Izzy took a deep breath and lowered her voice. "There's more. You umm... kind of... did it... umm invisibly."

"What?!" Conner yelled. Then he looked around. "Oops, sorry."

"He did?" Jake asked.

"Yeah. And then he appeared behind me, Thomas got up, and I punched him in the face. Thomas, not Conner."

"Order up for Jake Mitchell!" somebody at the counter yelled.

"Yep!" Jake shouted, walking up to grab their ice cream.

"So I can turn invisible," Conner whispered as if he didn't believe it.

"Yeah, and let's go somewhere a little more private," Izzy muttered.

They each took their ice cream from Jake and walked to Mittineague Park which took about five minutes. They walked in silence finishing their ice cream cones. They sat under a huge oak tree. "So, Conner, you can turn invisible now?" Jake asked.

"I guess? I don't know. I didn't feel invisible."

"Well you were," Izzy said.

"Wait," Jess said, "If you saw Conner, just *appear* out of thin air, did anyone else?"

"Umm I don't think so," Izzy said, though she didn't sound so sure. "I mean, nobody else seemed to notice that anything was wrong. Thomas just looked angry and scared. Everybody else was just looking at us, like they finally saw something entertaining, same as they always are when somebody starts a fight."

They all sat there thinking about how their lives had taken such a strange turn in the past months. It all started with Jake. Then Conner, and Izzy, and then Conner again. If Jess got a power what would it be? Would she get a superpower? Would any of them lose their powers? Or would they get more? They had so many questions and nobody to answer them.

"So Jake," Izzy said, changing the subject, "What do you wanna do for your birthday?"

Jake had completely forgotten that it was his birthday next week. "Nothing much. Maybe just going somewhere to eat. Like Wendys or something."

"Oh come on Jake! It's your sixteenth birthday! It's supposed to be special!" Conner said.

"We could have a party," Jess suggested.

"No way. What if I get mad, or Izzy, or Conner? We could hurt somebody."

"Who's going to make you mad at a birthday party? Come on Jake! Please?" Izzy begged.

"Fine," Jake agreed, reluctantly.

"Yes!" Jess said. "I'm going to invite all my friends, Izzy can invite her soccer team, and Conner can invite his baseball team!"

"What about *my* friends?" Jake said.

"Yeah I guess they can come," shrugged Jess, teasing.

"Where are we going to find a place big enough for all these people?" Izzy asked. "I mean I have fifteen people on my soccer team, so does Conner on his baseball team, Jess has, like, forty people that she's inviting. Jake's going to invite like fifteen people. So that's, if I'm doing the math right . . . eight-five people!"

"Well a sweet sixteen has to be big!" said Jess.

"Yeah I know, but if we don't have enough money to rent out a place like that, then we're just getting take-out or something," Jake said.

"Sure," Izzy said.

Jess started looking up stuff on her phone. "The Dante Club's having a really good discount. On Friday the fifteenth it's only thirty dollars to stay there and another hundred for food. I think we have a hundred thirty dollars to spare. How about we each pay forty three dollars and I'll just pay forty four. That way Jake doesn't have to pay anything and who doesn't want a Friday night party? Then we can just celebrate your actual birthday together, on Sunday."

Jake thought. Then he sighed and looked at his siblings. "Umm okay. But, I am *definitely* paying for something."

"No *way*, Jake. It's your birthday. You're not supposed to do anything except have fun and let us handle everything," Conner said.

"Exactly," Izzy agreed.

Jake looked like he wanted to argue, but Jess said something first, "Jake you've been working so hard. Let us do something for *you* for once okay?"

"Fine."

Chapter Nine

Jess said she had to go shopping for something to wear for the party at the mall and Conner and Izzy came too, so they could pick out a present for Jake. Jake had to go to a charity event with one of his clubs, so they didn't have to leave him alone all day. Conner got the first book in the Twilight series, which Jake really wanted to read. And afterwards Conner would get to read it too.

Izzy got him an Amazon gift card, along with a collar and leash for Otis. By the time they were done Jess was still trying on dresses. She finally chose a short, bright red dress, with a denim jacket. It cost most of the money she had, but she had a stash just for her siblings' presents. She got Jake a big binder so he could organize all his club meets, homework and any other activities he wanted to include in it.

Jess insisted that Izzy try on a dress, but she refused. Izzy told her she and her soccer team had already said that they were just going to wear their jerseys. Once she said no, Jess started harping on Conner, but he declined too. They ate at the mall and got back home around one. Jake said he would be home around one thirty, so they had time to wrap their presents. After that was done Izzy tried to give Otis a bath and Jake came home. Otis liked getting water all over Izzy more than he liked going in himself.

At one point Edel came in and demanded to give him a bath herself. Izzy let her, but Otis struggled so much that Edel just managed to get herself soaked. After she said he was clean, Izzy gave him an actual bath, and then put his new collar on him. Izzy, Conner, and Jess had hidden Jake's presents downstairs under a table and he was none the wiser. He thought they stayed home all day.

The next week at school nothing super eventful happened. Thomas was a jerk (no surprises there), but most people were talking about the huge party that the Mitchell's were throwing at the Dante Club. Friday came and all the siblings could do was think about the party.

While at school, they would look at the clock every five minutes to find it had barely changed at all. Finally it was three and the siblings took the bus home. The party started at five, so Jess started to get ready as soon as they got home. Ms. Mafore was sitting in her room watching television so the siblings wouldn't have to be that quiet to sneak out.

Edel was trying to play with Otis in her room, but she had forgotten to close the door, so Otis squirmed out of her hands and ran into Izzy. "Hey buddy," Izzy said, scratching him behind the ears. "Do you want to come with us to the party?" He barked and started chasing his tail. Izzy laughed, "I'll take that as a yes."

At four thirty Jess came back into the room with makeup, her dress and jacket, and her long black hair tied in a delicate braid down her back. "Jess you do know it's summer right?" Izzy asked. Izzy had changed into her soccer jersey and put her hair up in a high ponytail. Conner and Jake just wore T-shirts and shorts.

"Yeah I do, but the jacket looks so *nice* with the dress!"

Izzy sighed and put a little tuxedo jacket she had found on a doll from Edel's room, onto Otis. He looked so cute!

"Come on, one of my friends is picking us up," Jess said.

"One of your friends has a driver's license?" Jake asked.

"Yeah, she's in the grade above you."

Right on time a car honked from outside. Izzy scooped Otis up and tip-toed out the house. Conner, Jake, and Jess followed. It was a truck, so Jess sat in the front with her friend, who was as dressed up as she was, and the rest of the siblings sat in the back. "Is that your puppy? He's *so* cute!" she said.

"Yeah, his name's Otis," Izzy replied.

"Aww! Hi Otis, my name's Sophia," reaching out to pet him. He wagged his tail and allowed it. "Do they allow dogs at the Dante Club?" Sophia asked.

"Probably not," Izzy said, "but I can sneak him in."

Sophia smiled and backed out the driveway. "So, happy birthday Jake!" Sophia said.

"Thanks," Jake said.

"Anytime," she said and started talking to Jess.

When they got to the Dante Club there was already a crowd of cars waiting outside. The siblings walked in and Jess paid the person at the desk. Inside was a huge banner with the words, "**HAPPY BIRTHDAY JAKE!**" in colorful letters. "Did you tell them it was my birthday?" muttered Jake.

"Obviously," Conner grinned.

All the people the siblings invited attended the party. In all it was around ninety people. Everybody spread around the room in groups and started doing their own thing. Jess and her friends were flirting with boys by the appetizers. Izzy and her soccer team were having a Fanta chugging contest, which Otis was participating in too. Jake was talking with his friends by the kitchen, while Conner was playing catch with a beach ball with his baseball team.

Everybody was having a good time, which usually meant something was going to happen. Was it going to be good or bad? Only time would tell. So far Izzy and Otis were winning the contest, and none of the baseball team had broken anything. Then suddenly Jess shrieked. Everybody fell silent and turned toward her.

Her eyes looked wild, and, for once, it looked as if she didn't want all the attention. "I have to go to the bathroom," she muttered, her voice an octave higher than usual. She ran in the direction of the bathroom and Izzy followed her. Which meant Otis was also going into the bathroom.

"Jess, are you okay?" Izzy asked anxiously, knocking on the stall door. Jess unlocked and came out.

"Izzy? Where did you go?"

"I'm right here."

Jess looked at the floor and screamed. Where Izzy had been was a lean, gray and white wolf that had the same Fanta can that Izzy had been using near its paw. Otis licked the wolf's face, and it quickly transformed back into Izzy. Her mouth hung open.

"What just happened?"

"Umm. . . you kinda. . . shapeshifted into a wolf and back?"

"Weird. I wasn't mad."

"What does that mean?"

"Well I thought our powers only came out when we were super mad."

Jess shrugged. "Maybe it's just when we have strong emotions. Because I was super happy."

"I think it was because I was super anxious—wait. You said you were super happy? Does that mean you have a power too?"

"Maybe. Can I ask you a favor?"

"Yeah."

"Think of something."

"Like what?"

"I dunno. Just concentrate on one thing."

Izzy thought.

"You're thinking about how great of a team you and Otis made at the Fanta chugging contest." Jess's nose wrinkled at the mental picture formed in Izzy's mind

Izzy stared, open mouthed at Jess. "How did you know?" she asked breathlessly.

"Because I can read your mind," Jess said, matter of factly.

"Woah. What am I thinking of right now?"

"You're thinking about how you can find out all of Ms. Mafore's secrets and finally get out of the house."

"Yes!" Izzy did a happy dance. "My sister is a mind reader! My sister is a mind reader!"

Jess shrugged modestly. "I guess."

"Well this is super cool! I mean, you can *read people's minds*. How cool is that?! As long as you respect their privacy of course," she added.

Jess grinned, "Yeah it is super cool."

"We have to tell Jake and Conner!"

"Yeah, but it's Jake's sweet sixteenth. We *have* to stay."

Just then there was a knock at the door, "Hey Jess? Iz? Are you okay in there?" Conner asked.

"Yeah we're fine," she answered.

"Okay, just making sure." They heard his footsteps retreat.

"You okay to come out?" Izzy asked her sister.

She nodded, "And I don't want to use these powers to get everyone's secrets. People deserve their privacy."

Izzy nodded, "Except for Ms. Mafore, right?"

Jess shook her head, "Everyone deserves their privacy. Even witches." She suddenly let out a sigh.

"What?" Izzy asked.

"It's gone. I can't tell what you're thinking of anymore."

Izzy groaned. "Oh well. Let's go before somebody else comes in."

They walked out and rejoined the party. Jess told everybody who asked if she was okay that she was, and she just had a little stomach ache. Separately to Conner and Jake, she told them that she discovered her power. She wouldn't tell them at the party but once they got home she would give them all the details. It was kind of hard to celebrate when you know your sister has a new superpower, but they managed. Everybody headed home around ten. Jess's friend, Sophia, gave them a ride home. They snuck back inside their room.

Fortunately Ms. Mafore didn't notice. And for once they had done something that was completely normal for a teen. They had snuck out to a party at night and snuck back in without anybody noticing. They crashed in their beds and slept until ten in the morning, completely forgetting Jess's power. They would have slept longer except someone was banging on their door.

Izzy rubbed her eyes and stretched. Conner yawned loudly. Jess kept on snoring, and Jake shook her awake.

"Are you brats up yet!? I have something I want to discuss with you!" came Ms. Mafore's unwanted voice.

"We're getting up, we're getting up," Conner grumbled.

"I expect you to be dressed in the dining room in two minutes!" she screeched.

Jake sighed, Conner and Izzy rolled their eyes in unison, while Jess started untangling her rats' nest of hair. They rushed downstairs and found Ms. Mafore and Edel sitting at the rickety dining table. She gestured for them to sit down. Edel slurped grossly on a lollipop. "I have been thinking that we could use some help around the house and I've decided you're the perfect people for the job. You will be expected to clean the bathrooms every week, make breakfast for Edel, which means not sleeping in late. You will make her lunch for school, mow the lawn, clean Edel's room every Monday and Friday, do the laundry, take out the trash, wipe down the house, and if I have a special request that doesn't need to be done more than once, you are expected to do that too." It was as if she was punishing them for things they couldn't control, or things that weren't their fault.

The siblings' mouths hung agape. "Are you kidding me!?" Izzy cried.

"Is that all?" said Conner sarcastically.

"Yes that is. And no I'm not kidding."

Edel slurped on her lollipop just as Otis trotted in the room. He ran up to Izzy and jumped on her lap. She scratched him behind the ears and quietly seethed. So did the rest of the siblings.

"I'm going to make a list of things I need you to do today and then I'm going to work," Ms. Mafore told them, heading in the direction of her room. The siblings were so mad it was a miracle a hurricane didn't suddenly come sweeping in or Izzy didn't turn into a chipmunk and start attacking Ms. Mafore.

It would be different if she was just asking them to help around the house. The fact they had to do chores that didn't have to be done was maddening. Why was she now asking them to do chores? Was she trying to make them mad? Did she already know about their powers? Edel got up, stuck her half-eaten lollipop on the counter and dragged Otis into her room by the collar.

"Hey!" Izzy protested.

"Mommy! Izzy won't let me play with Otis!"

"Isabella, take your hands off that dog or I'll have you doing other chores too!" Ms. Mafore screeched.

So Izzy watched as Edel dragged Otis to her room with him protesting and whining the whole time. Jake started making breakfast while Jess got out plates, napkins, and silverware. Conner got drinks while Izzy made toast. Soon they each had a plate full of scrambled eggs and two pieces of toast. Sure, the bread was a bit stale, but you get what you get, right? Jake gave Izzy extra scrambled eggs, because he knew Otis would want some. And it's not like Ms. Mafore buys dog food.

Sometime during breakfast Otis made his way back to the siblings. He hopped on Izzy's lap and then onto the table, lapping up some of her orange juice and eating her eggs. They worked out a system. Otis would take a bite, then Izzy. Izzy would take a sip of OJ, then Otis. It was kinda gross, but whatever. She didn't care. They all finished breakfast then ran to their room to talk about what happened last night.

"Okay guys, what the heck happened last night?" Conner asked.

Jess shrugged. "I figured out my power."

"Well, what is it?" Jake said.

"I can read people's minds."

"What? Really? What am I thinking?" Conner asked.

"I dunno."

"Did somebody make you mad?" Jake asked.

"That's what I said! But no, Jess figured something out. It happens when you have strong emotions. Jess was super happy when she was reading minds. And I was super anxious when I turned into a wolf," Izzy said.

"*You turned into a wolf!?* So can you shapeshift into any type of animal? Did you want to attack something or somebody? Did you have a wolf's mind?" Conner asked.

"Well I did have this really big craving for raw meat, but other than that? No. I still felt like Izzy. Not a wolf."

"And she could speak like a regular human, not a wolf."

"That's kinda weird," Jake commented.

"Why wouldn't you be able to, like, speak wolf or something?" Conner asked.

"Maybe if you concentrated while in wolf form, or any animal, you could speak their language," Jess speculated. "Wait, how do bees communicate with each other?"

"Pheromones," Jake answered.

"Oh. I thought it was by dancing."

"If that does happen, will you have to learn their language, or will it just naturally come to you?" Conner said.

Izzy shrugged, lying on her back with Otis on her stomach.

"Okay since that's sorted out, I guess we have to do Ms. Mafore's chores," sighed Jess.

Jake and Izzy groaned in unison.

"What if we didn't do them? I mean she can't force us. Can she?" Conner said.

Jake shrugged. "She could tell Dr. Miao where we are."

"Was she bluffing though?"

"I don't think so," Izzy said.

Chapter Ten

The siblings celebrated Jake's birthday the next day after all their chores were done. While Ms. Mafore and Edel were out, Jess and Izzy made a huge birthday cake. Conner distracted and stalled Jake in their room. Izzy and Jess had made a three layer marble cake with blue frosting. Izzy, ever the artist, made a bunch of lifelike decorations out of fondant.

The one that took up most of the cake was a carving of the four siblings. They were all standing next to each other laughing and smiling. Surrounding it were a bunch of separate pictures. One was Otis. In a different one was what Izzy pictured would happen when Jake went to college.

In the picture, Jess was cleaning the apartment, while Conner and Izzy were trying to keep Otis away from the shoes and the cat that lived next door. Jake was trying to do his homework while laughing at Izzy and Conner. In the last picture Jake was smiling. He was in fifth grade and had short spiky hair with blue and white tips.

Every time any of the siblings saw that they burst out laughing. He looked so funny. Wearing a Star Wars shirt and sporting a crazy hair style. He was tall then. Five foot five. Now he was over six feet. Conner was five foot nine, Izzy five foot seven, and Jess five foot eight. They were a weirdly tall family. Once the cake was done Conner let Jake out and they all sat around the table.

Once Jake saw the cake he started crying and laughing at the same time. "Jake? What's wrong?" Izzy asked.

"Nothing Iz, this is an amazing cake." He gave her a hug. Jess looked outside just in time to see the clouds clear up, the sun come out, and a rainbow to appear. Her mouth dropped open. Then she smiled. Jake must've been really happy. And they all liked seeing that. Each of the siblings had two pieces of cake and then hid the rest in the hidden refrigerator compartment. After that they went to their room so Jake could open his presents.

He opened Conner's first. "This is awesome Conner! I really wanted to read this!" Then Izzy's. "Thanks Iz! I already know exactly what I'm buying." And last Jess's. "Cool Jess! Now I can organize all my classes and clubs." After he opened all of them he wrapped up Izzy, Conner, Jess, and Otis in a hug. Otis enjoyed it thoroughly and licked Jake's face several times. "Thanks so much guys."

"You're welcome Jake. We just wanted you to be happy on your birthday," Conner said.

"Well I'm really happy."

"Yeah, we know. It also shows in the weather."

For the first time, Jake, Conner, and Izzy looked outside. "I thought it was raining," Izzy said. "It *was*. But then Jake was super happy, and it shows," Jess explained, gesturing at the windows.

Izzy and Conner grinned. They loved it when *they* got the chance to make Jake happy, instead of the other way around. The rest of the day went unusually well for the siblings. They walked around the park and on top of having cake, they had ice cream. When they got home they saw Ms. Mafore's car in the driveway, which spoiled their spirits, but only a little.

They walked around the neighborhood until dark, and when the siblings walked inside, Ms. Mafore put down the phone, her face white. "Happy Birthday Jacob," she said with as little enthusiasm she could muster, her teeth clenched. The siblings exchanged surprised glances. Edel walked in, spotted Otis behind Izzy and rushed to him.

"Edel, honey, wish Jacob a happy birthday," Ms. Mafore said.

Her mouth fell open. The siblings were stunned. Never, in their fourteen years living there had Ms. Mafore even *acknowledged* any of their birthdays'! She almost *never* made Edel do anything that she didn't want, and by the look she was giving her mother, she definitely didn't want to. She whipped her head from side to side, indicating that she would *never* do something like that.

"Edel, do as your mother tells you!"

That's when the siblings' mouths fell open. Ms. Mafore never, not in a million years, raised her voice at her Edel! She glared at her mother nastily, but Ms. Mafore wouldn't budge. Then, forcing the words out. "Happy birthday Jake." She gagged and ran to her room. Ms. Mafore looked at the siblings distastefully. Then she too went into her room.

The siblings were too stunned to move. They looked at each other. "Did that really just happen?" Izzy asked.

"I think it did," Conner said, breathlessly.

"Hmm… " Jess said thoughtfully.

"What?" Izzy asked.

"Why'd she look so scared after the phone call? You don't think she was talking to Dr. Miao, do you?"

Jake shook his head. "She wouldn't have said happy birthday. She also made Edel say it, which was crazy. I think it was someone else."

"But who?" Conner said.

"Does it matter? I'm starving," Izzy complained.

Jess sighed. "I guess not. But I would like to meet the person who can scare the heck out of Ms. Mafore."

Conner agreed. "Me too."

Izzy opened the fridge and turned around, her mouth full of leftover pasta. "I guess

I would." She swallowed. "But what good would that do us?"

Jess started walking to their room. "We could use the person to scare Ms. Mafore out of the state."

Jake and Conner followed as Izzy trailed behind with the whole bin of pasta. They found Jess sitting down at her makeup table. "Do any of you guys want dinner before I eat it all?" Izzy asked.

"You have an endless stomach," Conner said, shaking his head.

"I do not! I'm just a growing female."

Conner rolled his eyes. "Nope I'm good."

"Jess, Jake? Want anything."

"Nah."

"No thanks."

Izzy nodded and continued shoveling food into her mouth. Jake helped Conner with his homework. And Jess just stared at herself in the mirror, criticizing every tiny detail, and then adding a bit of makeup here and there. "I don't know if you guys noticed, but I think I'm going to lay off boyfriends for a while."

Izzy looked up. "Yeah. I think it's going pretty well Jess. And. . . um. . ." She squirmed in her chair. "Thanks."

Jess smiled. "For what?"

"For being here more," Izzy said uncomfortably.

Jessica spun around her seat, walked over to Izzy, and gave her a huge hug. "I'll always be here for you guys," she whispered.

"I know," Izzy said, hugging her back tightly.

Conner quietly snapped a photo with his phone. He needed to have this for the next time they started arguing. Jess gently pulled away and went back to experimenting with makeup. Just then Otis trotted in. Izzy scooped him up and walked around the room with him. She took out her phone, put on her music, and promptly started dancing. Jess started humming along and soon Conner and Jake joined in too.

In five minutes they were all dancing around the room, singing at the top of their voices. At one point Otis joined in too, barking and howling. Then they were all on the floor, laughing and having a good time. It's a shame that almost every time the siblings have fun, Edel or Ms. Mafore has to ruin it. Ms. Mafore stormed in, her face tinged red.

"I was in the middle of a nap! Do you know how hard it is to find peace around here! Stop it this instant or I'll. . . I'll. . ." she stuttered off, her face growing pale. "Nevermind. Go on." And she left the room. The siblings didn't feel like worrying about it now, so they focused on more happy things. Like right now.

The next day was pretty boring. Since it was so late in the school year, they really didn't do anything. Whatever fear had made Ms.

Mafore be more polite than usual, had disappeared, if anything she was more nasty than usual.

That Wednesday was their last day at school. Izzy and Conner had the worst teacher, who gave them a huge packet that had to be finished by the end of the day. The packet quizzed them on everything that they had learned during the year, down to which Social Studies project they did on which day. Jess had one of the best teachers. He let them use their phones and do whatever they wanted for the whole day.

Once school was out, the siblings walked over to Coach's to have a "healthy lunch," made up entirely of ice cream, paid for by the stolen money out of Ms. Mafore's purse. Conner got three scoops of chocolate, with chocolate sprinkles, and hot fudge, in a chocolate waffle cone. Izzy called it the "Conner Special." Jess got a scoop of fat free vanilla with rainbow sprinkles. Jake got three scoops of cookie dough with hot fudge, in a bowl.

Izzy, by herself, got two humongous orders. One scoop of chocolate, two scoops of brownie blast, and another two scoops of cookies and cream. She added three squirts of hot fudge, a bunch of sour gummy worms, and three dollops of whipped cream. On the second order she got three scoops of New York Cheesecake, three scoops of strawberry, and two scoops of cookie dough. To top it off, she got three cherries, ten mini marshmallows, and a handful of Reese's Pieces.

Once they finished (Izzy also stealing a bite from each of her siblings in turn) they fed and took Otis on a long walk. It was a pretty good last day of school. Well, for the siblings anyway. Edel was very, *very* angry when they got home. And it was because her teacher had written a note home. It was about how she was being rude to her classmates, not listening to any of the teachers, and getting almost all failing grades.

Ms. Mafore went to the school to complain that Edel just needed special attention, and that she was just being rude to her classmates because they were rude to her first. Conner went to the town library right after they got back from walking Otis. He said he wanted to have enough books for the first month of summer. He came back home with over twenty books, most of them being ones he already read.

During the second day of summer vacation was when it happened. Conner was reading, Izzy was drawing, Jess was texting, and Jake was also reading. Conner let out a very loud, startled yell. "What?!" Jake asked. "What happened?"

Conner turned to look at him, white faced. "This book," he whispered, and the rest of the siblings leaned in, barely able to hear him.

"What about it?" said Jess.

"The story. It's about... it's about," he looked around to make sure no one was around, and lowered his voice even farther. "It's about us."

"What do you mean *about us*?" Jess asked.

"It tells about what we are, and. . . well I haven't got that far, I'm still in the first chapter."

"Let me see it," Jake said, calmly.

Conner tossed the book to him and Jake looked at it's cover. It was kind of old-fashioned, leather bound, with shimmering, golden words, etched into its surface. *The Tale of the Animagee.* Jake flipped through it, stopping when he saw a part where the words jumped out at him. *Animagee will start to experience strange and unusual powers at an early age. Although each Animagee is different, some examples might include, talking to animals, reading thoughts, or minds, creating energy*

*fields, or expanding the body. Most of the time,
these special powers will come out when the
Animagee in turn are feeling very strong
emotions. As said, this happens to each
Animagee at a different time, from years 3-7.*

Jake went pale. "It . . . it is about us," he
muttered, mostly to himself. "Just, the timing is
off."

"Read the first page, Jake," Conner told
his older brother, his voice never going above a
whisper. "Read it."

Jake flipped to the introductory
paragraph. *If you are able to see 'The Tale of the
Animagee' on the cover of the book, then
congratulations! You are Animagee! This
means you have special blood in your veins
that allows you to do what regular humans
have only dreamed of doing: performing
magic. Or, having "super powers." To regular
humans this would look like a regular book.*
Jake stopped reading.

"What? What does it say?" Izzy demanded, leaning so far out of her chair that she fell out of it and onto the floor.

Jake read the first passage aloud. Jess and Izzy's mouths fell open. "Do you think there are more of us? Like the book said?" Jess asked, breathlessly, but her younger sister was skeptical.

"What do they mean humans can't see? How would they not be able to see it? How do they know that we have powers? Can they be trusted? Who's the author?"

Conner struggled to remember all of her questions. "I don't know. I don't know again. I still don't know. I really can't answer these questions, Izzy! I just found out about this book!" He grabbed the book back from Jake to look at the author. "Eliza Kerrie."

Izzy glanced at her siblings. "Do any of you know who she is?"

Conner shook his head. So did Jake and Jess. "Should we go ask Ms. Mafore if she can read it, or see what it says?"

Jake shrugged. "Sure."

Conner ran out of the room, his three siblings trailing behind him. "Ms. Mafore!" Conner said, skidding to a stop.

Ms. Mafore was in the kitchen chopping vegetables for lunch.

"What?" she snapped, turning around to face the siblings.

Izzy showed her the book. "What's this say?" Izzy asked, elbowing her way in front of her twin.

Ms. Mafore's eyes skimmed the cover, then looked back at the siblings. "Why? Can't you read?"

Conner looked around at his siblings, trying to silently ask them for help. Jess thought of something quick. "Yeah, but it's in cursive, and they didn't teach us it in school yet."

"Of course they taught you cursive! Don't play dumb with me."

"Yeah, but I slept through that class." *That* wasn't much of a lie.

"Then ask your brother Jacob. I bet *he* didn't, that teacher's pet."

"He doesn't remember."

Ms. Mafore squinted at the book cover. "It's one of your Harry Potter books, is it not? I would think you would be able to recognize it."

But the siblings were already racing back toward their room. "Well? *Well?!*"

"Well what Conner? It's an actual book. So what. It doesn't really make that much of a difference. We knew we were different. We knew we were special. The book doesn't tell us anything that we don't already know," Jess said.

"Harsh, Jess," Conner muttered.

Jess rubbed her eyes. "I'm sorry Conner. I just don't see how this puts us into a better place than we were half an hour ago."

"Let me read through all of it. Then we can talk about whether it matters or not," Conner said, slipping into his bunk bed and starting to read. The others went back to their activities, but it was pretty hard to focus.

Chapter Eleven

The siblings waited impatiently for Conner to finish. They skipped lunch, except for Izzy who took some and brought it into their room. "Done!" Conner announced looking up from the last page of the book. Izzy stopped with a spoonful of soup on the way to her mouth, Jake stopped mid sentence, and Jess hung up on her friend, which was pretty rude.

"So, what's it say?" Jess asked impatiently.

Conner was practically glowing with happiness. Then he disappeared. "Conner?" Izzy called out. "Where'd you go?"

"I'm right here," he said, from the spot where he had been sitting.

"Umm, no you're not," Jake said, looking around.

"*BOO!*" came a loud voice from behind Izzy. She jumped about a foot in the air.

"*Conner!*" she shrieked. "Don't *do* that!"

Conner appeared behind Izzy, holding his sides. He was laughing so hard.

"So," Jake said, redirecting the conversion. "What happened in the book?"

Conner took a deep breath, calming himself down. He took a seat down next to Izzy, who promptly hit him. "Jerk."

Jess rolled her eyes at her younger siblings. "Go on."

Conner collected himself, and then turned invisible again. "Conner! Stop doing that!" Izzy said.

"Sorry! I can't control it. I guess I'll have to tell you like this. So, there are more people like us. In fact," he took a deep breath. "There's a whole entire *kingdom* of Animagee."

This was followed by the loud voices of his siblings. "*What?* A whole *kingdom*?" Jake asked.

"Really?" Jess said, trying to be heard over Jake's voice.

But Izzy had the loudest vocal cords of everyone. "WHERE?!"

"I don't know. I didn't want to read the map yet."

"Well then read it!" Jess said. She had run out of patience.

They heard footsteps walk over to Conner's bed. The sound of flipping pages filled the silent air. "Got it," he said, breathlessly.

"Can I see it?" Jake asked.

"Conner, it might be better if you turned visible," Jess told her younger brother.

Conner concentrated, then popped back into existence.

"Here," he said, passing the book to Jake.

Jake opened the book. It showed two blank pages.

"Conner, there's still nothing there," Izzy said.

"Yeah there is!"

The rest of the siblings concentrated, but nothing happened.

"Okay. . . Well it's not showing up for us," Jake said.

"It's literally right there."

"It's literally not," Izzy argued.

"Yeah it is! Look, there's four dots that probably represent us, then it has a bunch of different houses and streets. It has a red line coming from us off the map. Actually hold on a sec." He grabbed the book back from Jake and ran out of the room.

"Conner!" Izzy yelled. "Get back here!"

Conner didn't stop. The siblings ran after him. Izzy, being the fastest, caught up to him in less than a minute. "What the heck are you doing? Stop running!"

But he wouldn't stop. Not until he got at least a mile away. "What the heck Conner!? What were you thinking?!"

He didn't say anything. He held the book open to the blank page, examining it. "Conner! Answer me!"

Conner looked at his twin. "It works," he said panting.

"What works? What are you talking about?"

"The map. It goes off the page."

"What's that supposed to mean?"

"It would be *so* much easier if you could see this."

"Conner?"

"What?"

"I can see it."

"Wait, really? What color are the dots?"

"Blue, red, green, purple."

"Yes! You can see it!"

"I know I can."

"But why?"

"Why what?"

Just then their older siblings ran up to them, panting. Well, initially it was only Jake wh ran up to them as Jess was still at least a good five minutes away. "What the heck Conner!? You don't just run off like that!"

"I had a good reason too!"

"Jake! Calm down. Concentrate. Try to imagine the map on the page."

Jake stared down at the blank pages. Suddenly he gasped.

"See it?"

"Yep."

The oldest sibling studied the map. It showed four colorful dots, which he figured represented them. The green, blue, and red dots stood in a small group. The purple dot trailed behind, moving rather slowly. A thick red line snaked from one end of the paper to the other. He guessed that represented the way towards the kingdom. The rest of it looked like a regular map, except unusually detailed.

Colorful buildings, houses, streets, parks, and forests were all lined up with perfect accuracy. Then it all disappeared. Izzy and Jake stared at the map in confusion. "What?" asked Conner. "What happened?"

"It all just disappeared," Jake said.

"And I got a really bad headache," Izzy added.

Jake was startled to realize that he did too. Before they could figure out what happened, Jess ran up, wheezing and holding her sides. She doubled over, and, in between gasps she yelled at Conner. "Conner! What the heck? DO YOU KNOW HOW HARD IT IS TO RUN IN HEELS!?"

Izzy covered her mouth, trying not to laugh. "What? What is it?" Jess asked.

In response Izzy pointed at Jess's hair in which a chipmunk had made itself at home. Jess started shrieking and screaming hysterically. Batting at her hair she yelled, "I HATE MY LIFE!"

She wacked the chipmunk, and it went sailing into the woods. "Jess calm down," Jake said.

"Calm down? *Calm down!? What do you mean* calm down!? How am I supposed to be calm? A chipmunk made itself comfy in my hair, I just ran a mile *in heels*, there's a whole kingdom of people like us, *people with powers*! Actual powers! Evil doctors trying to kill us, a disgusting little brat that we have to share a home with! So I swear to god, Jacob Blake Mitchell DON'T TELL *ME* TO CALM DOWN!"

Jake was taken aback. Izzy and Conner stared at Jess, looking almost identical with the same expressions on their faces. Expressions of surprise, fear, and a bit of awe. They had never seen Jess get *this* mad, or hysterical. She was practically steaming and crying at the same time. Jake walked over to her, then gave her a tight, comforting hug.

"I know Jess. This sucks. But it's our life now. We have to deal. It's the only way. Now please, chill. Conner has some important information."

He gently pulled away, as Jess quickly wiped at her eyes. She was embarrassed of her meltdown. Embarrassed and ashamed. She didn't want her younger siblings to see, so she quickly turned away. "Umm... yeah. So, Conner, we can't see the map anymore," Izzy said, redirecting the conversation.

"I think it has something to do with our headaches," Jake added.

Conner nodded. "It doesn't really matter, as long as one of us can see it. So, what I was trying to accomplish by running a mile is seeing if this map will go in different directions."

"Huh?"

Conner sighed. "It only shows a limited amount of space. About half a mile in each direction because it's so detailed. I wanted to know if it'll keep going. It does, but the land behind us will disappear. Before I could see the school, but I couldn't see the park. Now, since I ran in the direction of the park, the school is gone."

Izzy nodded. "Oh. I guess that makes sense. How far does it go?"

Conner shrugged. "I don't know, but I'm guessing the red line shows where the place is."

They all started to walk back home, still talking. "How far away do you think it is?" Jess asked.

"Conner, you can't seriously be considering going there."

"Yes, Izzy. I am."

"But we don't even know if the author is lying or not! What if they're evil like Dr. Miao?

What if they wanna cut us up and do experiments on us?"

Out of nowhere, Jake came up with a sudden realization. "*Eliza Kerrie*. We *do* know her!"

"We do?" Conner asked.

Jake sighed. "*You* two don't. Jess and I do."

"Amelia Heart! *Eliza Kerrie is Amelia Heart!*" Jess said.

"How'd you figure that out?" Izzy asked.

Jess and Jake shrugged in unison. "I don't know. But it feels right."

Jess nodded. "It does."

"I mean, who else could it be?" Jake said. "Dr. Miao didn't seem to want us to know what we are. You remember the way he was talking? I wish we could just figure out *how* we could know for sure."

Izzy shrugged. "Let's do an internet search."

They ran the rest of the way home. Once they got there, they found Otis whining and scratching at the door. "It's okay buddy," Izzy said, picking him up. "You can come on our other adventures."

Otis wagged his tail and barked happily. The siblings raced towards their room. Jake skidded inside, grabbing his computer. He flipped it open and started typing madly.

"Well?" Izzy asked impatiently.

"Hang on. It's gotta load."

They waited for what seemed like forever. Then a bunch of pictures and websites started popping up. "Click on images," Conner said, hovering over Jake's shoulder.

Jake clicked. A ton of images popped up, of all different people. "I see her!" Jess gasped. Jess was right. In the center of the page, an older woman smiled mischievously at them. In the background, they could just make out the blurry image of a castle. "It can't be," Izzy whispered. "It can be photoshopped, right?"

Conner nodded. "It can, but I don't think it is."

Jess and Jake didn't think so either. "It just. . . I feel like I've seen it before."

Conner looked at his older brother curiously. "Really?"

Jake nodded. "Yeah, but I must've been super young."

Izzy shook her head. "But I thought we've been here our whole lives?"

Jake and Jess shook their heads. "I don't think so," Jess said.

Izzy and Conner's mouths fell open again. "What? That's impossible. We've been here our whole lives! That's what Ms. Mafore said."

"Are you really going to believe *her*, Izzy? After all the things she lied about? All the things she *did*?" Jess said.

Izzy sighed. "I guess not. But, we could've gone on *vacation*, or. . . or. . ." she struggled to think of something else.

"Or nothing Izzy," Jake said gently. "We've never been on vacation here. We've never even been out of the state."

Exactly!" Izzy said. "We've never been out of the state, so how could we have ended up in a kingdom for people with powers when we were little?"

Jake sighed. "I just *know* Izzy. We've been there. Jess and I at least."

Conner nodded. "I think it makes sense. But the real question is, are we gonna go?" The siblings pondered this the whole next day. Jess and Conner were in favor, Jake was on the fence, and Izzy wanted nothing to do with it, which was strange since she was the one who wanted to run away in the first place. This was a perfect opportunity, but she didn't want to take it. Otis, however, was the opposite. When the siblings had discussed leaving, he was barking and wagging his tail happily.

Two days later Jake called a family meeting. They all gathered around the coffee table. Izzy laid a platter of sugar cookies in the middle, along with some milk. Otis grabbed one with his teeth, although nobody else did. "So," Jake said. "We are all gathered here today to discuss the problem of well... I don't really know how to explain. I guess I'll put it like this, do we really want to go on a risky adventure to who knows where for an unknown period of time to try and find people like us?

"To clarify, people with powers. This has to be a unanimous decision. Everybody will get their own turn to speak. I'll start. First, I think that this could be a trap. We don't even know Eliza Kerrie or Amelia Heart, whichever, or if she's got our best interests at heart. All we know is that she wrote this book," he gestured to *The Tale of the Animagee*. "And we saw her at the hospital. I also think this could be our one chance to find out what's happening to us, and possibly find more people who can help us. Conner, you're up."

"Okay. I think that it's a great opportunity to find out more about us, where we came from, and what's happening to us. The people there, in the kingdom, could help us learn to control our powers. We could be *happy* there. It's not like we've got anything to lose. Jess."

Jess had been nodding along with what Conner had said. "What he said. Izzy."

Izzy rolled her eyes. "This is a terrible idea. It's *obviously* a trap, and even if it isn't, well how do we know that these people want us? We don't. They could just kick us out and then where would we go? Back here? No. Way. It'll be so much better and save us the humiliation if we just stay here. Otis."

Otis went over and sat down between Conner and Jess. He barked, and then looked back and forth between Conner and Jess.

"Traitor," Izzy muttered.

"OK," Jake said, "Now we vote. If you would like to say something else along with your vote, go ahead. But make it quick, Ms. Mafore and Edel should be coming back in about twenty minutes. I'll go last. Conner?"

"I vote yes. We should go. Doing this is better than sitting around here for the rest of our lives." He looked pleadingly at Izzy. "Jess."

"I vote yes. This is our one chance to find out who we are. Who we *really* are. Izzy."

Izzy took a deep breath, and thought for a bit, looking torn. She bit her lip. "I vote. . ."

Chapter Twelve

"Yes. I vote yes. Jake."

Conner and Jess grinned. Otis barked with joy and hopped into Izzy's lap. Jake smiled.

"I vote yes too." The room erupted in cheers. "It's a unanimous decision. We leave in two days. If anyone has any objections, speak now or forever hold your peace." Otis barked. "Oh right. Otis? Bark once if you want to stay here, twice if you want to leave." Otis barked twice. "OK then. Guys, start packing. We leave Friday. But first, group hug."

They all hugged each other. Otis barked and licked everybody's face at least five times. Then they heard the front door open. "We're home!" Ms. Mafore announced from the kitchen. "And I've decided that you brats will be making dinner for us all. I'm much too tired."

The siblings were too excited to argue. They walked out to the kitchen and started making pasta. Well, Izzy made the food. Jake got drinks, Conner set the table, and Jess sat around talking. Ms. Mafore went to her room, while Edel watched television in the living room. The siblings had to endure several episodes of My Little Pony while making pasta.

They finally finished. Edel insisted that she be able to watch My Little Pony while eating her dinner, so she and Ms. Mafore ate in the living room while the siblings ate in their room. They were silent as they ate, contemplating what had happened a mere hour before. That one decision was going to change their lives forever. They just didn't know if it was gonna be good or bad yet.

The next day they started preparing for what might be a very long journey. They each dumped out their school backpacks and started filling them with their most valuable things. Jess packed her best makeup kit and one of her favorite posters of actor, Thomas Brodie Sangster. Izzy packed her signed soccer ball, sketchpad, colored pencils, and a leash with dog bags for Otis. Conner packed three books and noise canceling headphones. Jake packed his best report cards, chromebook, a couple of blank notebook pages, his binder (he wasn't ready to forget it), and the Twilight series book that Conner had gotten him.

They were going to pack food tomorrow, so it would be as fresh as possible. In a suitcase they packed clothes, toiletries, and money. They grabbed one more backpack that they planned to fill with food. They slept until nine o'clock the next morning, knowing it would be a long day. They planned to leave around eleven the next morning because that was when Ms. Mafore and Edel were leaving to go to the park.

They packed anything that would last them a pretty long time and didn't need an oven to be cooked. They would still get fast food, but it was better to be safe than sorry. Izzy went into Ms. Mafore's room and grabbed all the money out of her wallet as a last thought.

They strapped sleeping bags and pillows to their backs, along with a backpack each. Izzy and Jake carried two backpacks. Conner had *The Tale of the Animagee* book out, while Jess walked Otis. They took one last, long look at the house. It didn't hold many good memories, but it was technically home, however much they wished it wasn't.

They turned around and none of them, not even Otis, gave a single glance back. About three hours later Conner said, "Okay, it's official. We're lost."

Izzy groaned. "I thought there was a red line or something."

"There *is*. We're on it. But it goes off the street."

They were on a sidewalk on a main street. Cars passed them. Behind the houses were mountains and forests. "Well, then follow it!" Izzy said. She wasn't the patient type.

Conner shrugged. "Fine. But can we eat first? We haven't had lunch yet."

Izzy nodded. "Yeah. I'm starving."

"Sure." Jake said. "Let's see what we have."

Izzy opened the backpack with the food. "We have some bread and peanut butter along with some chips."

"What about water?" Conner asked.

Jake groaned. "*That's* what I forgot. Water."

"No you didn't. I have some in here." Jess pulled out some water from her backpack. Izzy started smearing peanut butter on bread. Jake filled a small bowl for Otis. Conner studied the map.

"It looks like the forest isn't actually that big and there's a clearing on the other side."

Izzy guzzled down her water and devoured her sandwich. Jess only finished half of hers, so she let Izzy have the rest. "Will we have to cross into somebody's yard to get to the forest?" Jess asked.

"Looks like it. I don't see another way. We'll run through this person's house. There's a white fence that'll open up to the forest. But we'll have to run in case there's somebody home, don't fall in the pool. Or run into the shed. Ready?"

Jess, Jake, Izzy, and Otis nodded. "Okay. Go NOW!" The siblings and Otis ran into the driveway, dodging a basketball hoop. They quickly opened the gate that led to the backyard. It had a pool straight in front of them, with a shed behind it. They were standing on an outdoor patio. "Over there!" Conner yelled.

They sprinted towards the shed, finding the gate behind it. They slammed it close behind them as they heard someone from the backyard yell, "HEY! Get back here!" They didn't stop until they were hidden by the forest. The siblings doubled over gasping for breath. They would've been out about five times faster if they hadn't been carrying such a heavy load.

"Can we take a break?" Jess asked.

"Sure," Jake said, sitting down.

They took a quick five minute break. Otis fell asleep on the ground and was snoring exceptionally loud. "Can we stay a bit longer? Just for, like, ten minutes?" Izzy asked. Jake nodded. Conner leaned against the tree, and Jess sat on the ground, gently petting Otis. Then Izzy jumped violently. "What?" Jake asked.

"Didn't you guys hear that?" she asked, her voice no more than a whisper.

"Hear what?" Jess asked.

Izzy went white. "That."

The rest of the siblings strained their ears. Otis had woken up at the sound of Izzy's voice, and now his fur was sticking straight up, and he was growling loudly. The bushes to the right of them rustled. They quickly grabbed their things and ran to the other side. Izzy had her hands clenched tightly, her eyes closed.

Each one of them tried to think of the most angering thoughts possible, just in case. "Come out!" Izzy yelled, bravely.

"I really don't think you would like that," came a frighteningly familiar voice. A figure walked out of the bushes, looking very evil holding two wicked looking daggers. The siblings stared into the face of Dr. Miao. "RUN!" Jake yelled. The siblings took off dumping their belongings. Otis raced beside Izzy. Dr. Miao snapped his fingers. A loud CRACK filled the forest and Izzy screamed and fell.

"Oh god, oh god. My leg!" she moaned, clutching her left shin in her hands.

Conner skidded to a stop and called out to Jake and Jess. Otis stood protectively in front of Izzy, barking at Dr. Miao. Fortunately Dr. Miao wasn't moving very fast, and he was panting. Conner ran to Izzy. "Iz? What is it? What happened?"

"My leg," Izzy said, her eyes tightly closed. "I think It's broken."

Jake and Jess arrived. "Okay," Jake said, trying to think of something. "I'll carry her. But we gotta go. I'll try and call a storm." He scooped Izzy up and carried her, bridal style. He started muttering in concentration. "Jake," Jess whispered as Conner hurried them along using the map. "He doesn't know where we went. He gave up. He's going back. We can stop running."

Jake didn't stop. The sky darkened. "Jake! Stop! He's gone!" Jess said, shaking him.

Jake's eyes snapped open and the sky went back to blue. "We're almost there," Conner said. "I can see where it ends."

"Guys? Wait up. I can't carry Izzy anymore." Jake collapsed on the ground. Otis leaped up on Izzy and started licking her.

Izzy whimpered. "Otis get off. . . *Otis*." Then, "Oh my god, Otis! What did you do?!"

Conner, Jess, and Jake spun around to face Izzy, who was up on her feet. Otis was snoring on the ground next to her. Izzy gathered him into her arms. "It's okay buddy. It's okay."

Conner's mouth hung open. "Did Otis just *heal you*? Did our dog just *fix your broken leg*?"

Izzy nodded. "By licking it," she informed him.

"Do you think *Otis* has a *superpower*?"

She shrugged. "Looks like it."

"*Looks like it? How are you not freaking out? The dog. . .*" he muttered. Then louder he sighed, "Let's go."

They kept walking, Izzy carrying Otis. "Wait, why aren't we running anymore?"

"Oh, I was able to read Dr Miao's mind. He went back. Then he thought something weird."

"What was it?" Jake asked.

"I don't know. It was some sort of jumbled, half-formed thought."

"But he's definitely gone?"

"Yes Iz, he's definitely gone."

Izzy gave a sigh of relief and cuddled Otis. "We're here!" Conner announced.

"But where is *here*?" Jess asked.

They had just stepped out of the forest and into a clearing. There was a huge oak tree next to a small lake with a waterfall running into it. "It's so pretty!" Jess gasped.

"So? Who cares if it's pretty? Where is it?"

Conner looked down at the map. "I guess it could be a bit farther."

They walked towards the large tree. "It should be right here! I don't get it."

Izzy sat down, leaning against the tree. "Where the heck is the entrance to Animagee Kingdom!?"

Suddenly there was a loud rumbling sound. "Earthquake?" Jess asked.

Jake shook his head. "Not in this area."

Suddenly the tree's trunk opened up. Izzy almost fell backwards. "Wha. . .?"

Inside of the tree trunk was a portal. "Well?" Conner asked.

"Well, what?" Jess said.

"*Well are we going to go into the secret portal hidden in a tree that hopefully leads to a kingdom with special people that have powers!?*"

"Oh, that. Obviously."

Chapter Thirteen

Izzy sighed. "Are we sure we want to do this?" she whispered. "I mean, it could put us in a worse place than we already are."

Jess shrugged. "I don't see how it could get any worse, and *no*, I *don't* want you to tell me how it could get worse," she added as Izzy opened her mouth.

Izzy glared at her older sister. "It could get a *lot* worse."

"I'm willing to take the chance," Jake said.

"So am I," Conner agreed.

Otis barked as Jess nodded.

Izzy let out a long, exaggerated groan. "Fine! But if we get killed I swear I'm gonna turn into a wolf and kick your butts'."

"Okay. Ready?" Jake asked, looking around at his siblings.

They all nodded, looking nervous. The siblings joined hands with Otis sitting on Izzy's shoulder. At the last second Izzy pulled away. "Are we *sure* we want to do this? Like, absolutely, positively sure?"

Jake nodded, looking exasperated. "Yes, Izzy. We are absolutely, positively sure. But are you?"

Izzy twisted her hands. "It's just. . . a month or two ago we were in high school, learning about things every other kid was. Now, here we are, four kids with superpowers, running away from evil doctors who want to experiment on us. Destroying schools and turning into wolves. Reading minds and becoming invisible. It's just a long leap from where we are. And, even if I don't act like it, I'm really, *really* scared." She looked down, embarrassed.

Conner hugged his twin. "So am I," he muttered quietly. "But I'd rather take this chance. I'd rather be able to turn into a wolf or destroy a building than be a normal person. Even if it comes with all this. . .," he struggled to find a word.

Izzy started crying on his shoulder. She took a couple deep breaths, trying to calm herself. "OK," she said. "I'm ready."

"Anybody else have any *confusing* feelings?" Jake asked. "Last time to say something."

"I do!" Jess said. "I just wanted to say that I'm sorry for anything I've ever done to hurt any of your feelings." Her eyes turned a little misty. "I love you guys."

"Same," Conner agreed. "I'm also sorry for ruining your clothes Jess. But it did look really funny when you walked into school and part of the backside of your pants were ripped!"

Jake and Izzy laughed, while Jess glared. "I love you guys too," Jake said after a minute.

They all hugged each other. Time passed. It might've been a minute , it might've been an hour. None of them wanted to be the first to pull away. Finally Jake untangled himself. "Ready?"

They all glanced at each other before linking hands. "Ready," they said in unison. Jake took a deep breath before leaping into the portal. Whatever happened they would get through it. And they would do it together.

.

Made in United States
North Haven, CT
11 March 2022